New case, new client.
Same hangover ...

It starts out as a simple maritime stalking case, which Banyon flat-out refuses. The would-be client is the god of the sea, see, and Crag Banyon is a strict reformed agnostic: while he believes in the existence of gods, he prefers it if they don't pester him during happy hour.

Unfortunately, something big is stirring offshore, the coast is being flooded, and despite his best efforts to stay planted on his favorite barstool, Banyon finds himself swept up in a case of Olympian intrigue, dirty deals and fresh fish. Soon he's up to his pretty little neck in trouble, paddling for his life, taking on water, and in the end it's either sink or swim.

Does it all come out in the wash? Just ask his secretary:

> *"Crag Banyon? That jerk's a bum,*
> *and that's the Gods' honest truth!"*

SEA NO EVIL

A Crag Banyon Mystery

JAMES MULLANEY

James Mullaney Books

Cover art: Scotty Phillips

Cover design/layout: Micah Birchfield

Interior design/layout: Rich Harvey

Copyright © 2013 by James Mullaney

Dedication

For the papergirl,
Peggy Mailloux

SEA NO EVIL

1

The windows were far too clean and there weren't any winos sleeping it off on the sidewalk out front, which were strikes one and two, respectively, against the too-tidy bar on the corner of St. Sodom's Boulevard and Donny Most Drive.

I don't trust people with clean windows.

Everybody who's honest has something to hide, even if it's just an overflowing cat box or a pile of unwashed dishes in the kitchen sink. Your eyes might be the windows to your soul, but your windows are the windows to a soiled laundry pile that's grown so massive you've had to carve tunnels through that mound of dirty underwear like one of those roads they hack through Sequoia trunks. Honest people aren't out with a bucket of suds and a squeegee every other day precisely because they're capable of embarrassment and are therefore ashamed of what you might see through a spotless picture window. It's a whole psychological thing. Trust me. It's my job.

On the other hand, it's the dishonest scumbags I've met who always put on the biggest show of having nothing to hide. And windows as spotless as the ones on The Seaweed Palace Bar virtually guaranteed the place was run by a tax cheat with a dozen lime-packed hookers wrapped in plastic shower curtains and shoved up in his crawlspace.

Lucky for me I'd quit the cops ten years ago, so whatever dirty little secrets the spotlessly clean windows were hiding were none of my business. But the lack of drunks snoozing on the grates out front was another matter altogether.

There was a time when I walked a beat as a rookie cop around that part of town. Back then I couldn't go ten feet without tripping over a supine sidewalk tippler. The area had gone upscale in the past couple of decades and I assume the first thing to get the heave-ho had been the bums. Call me sentimental, but I prefer a sloppy sidewalk drunk mangling "Danny Boy" while pissing his pants in the gutter to a prissy yuppie belting out show tunes behind the wheel of a Chevy Volt. Hippie hybrid bastards.

I'd been up late the previous night on a bender of my own, so my gin-soaked nostalgia that afternoon made me hope that the sidewalk winos from way back in the day had merely taken a five minute break to stumble inside for a bowl of free soup and a bottle of cheap muscatel. Or maybe a gang of baristas armed with push brooms from the Starbucks next door to The Seaweed Palace Bar had swept them into the canal. If that was the case there were a lot of unlucky boozed-up bastards bobbing around like stewed corks in the harbor. Everyone with a brain was steering clear of the water these days.

The ocean had been going crazy as hell the past couple of weeks. It was all over the news. The storms out at sea had shaken up the ocean floor like a snow globe filled with lobster traps and medical waste.

A storm surge the previous day had dumped a bunch of flapping green sea monsters onto dozens of estates out on ritzy Spoke Island. Between the doe eyes and the cooing sound they made, everyone thought they were cute as all hell. The love-fest lasted only until the fangs came out. At least the feel-good summer movie that might have come from it died the minute one of them ate Steven Spielberg in his driveway. Little bugger swallowed Kate Capshaw too. There's always a silver lining.

A deep-sea Leviathan had wandered into the harbor and had been lazily pulling apart tugboats and slapping the pieces around with its tentacles since Friday.

Everybody near the shore was most concerned about some haunted pirate fog that had been floating around nights just after dusk. Some junked ship with a royally pissed-off dead man crew had been choking people up and down the coast, I guess to remind them to properly weather-strip their windows. Who knows? Goddamned ghosts.

Lucky for me my two feet were firmly on dry land. I'd only ventured that close to the harbor that particular afternoon because I had a meeting with a client. My name's Banyon. I'm a P.I. It said so on the faded yellow card I had stashed in one of my pockets somewhere, although I didn't take it out much because it was the only one I owned. It was like the Constitution. If I'd had the dough, I'd've put it under glass in my office.

Speaking of glasses, closing time had been hours before and if I was going to get through a business meeting I'd need a full one in front of me.

I tipped back the brim of my fedora and strolled through The Seaweed Palace's too-clean front door.

The joint called itself a bar but it smelled like a hayloft

and looked like one of those dirt-free plastic rooms where they make computer chips. The tables and chairs were white plastic teardrops which were suffering from the same unhealthy bout of cleanliness that afflicted the windows. The bar was some kind of stainless steel and vinyl chimera, like the ugly accident that came nine months after a DeLorean spent a wild weekend in Cabo with a cheap office couch. The woman behind the bar was as cheerful as I wasn't, and when she flashed her bright Stepford smile I wished I'd brought my sunglasses so I could stuff them down her throat.

"Good morning, sir, would you like to see a menu?" she asked, oozing more syrup than Mrs. Butterworth with a bellyful of buckshot.

Strike one. Bars need menus like airplanes need orchestras.

"Just give me your biggest glass filled with your brown-est liquid and a bowl of your least stale pretzels," I said.

"Oh, we don't have pretzels," she said with a sympathetic V in her brow that was in direct opposition to the gleaming grin that never left her ruby lips.

As she spoke, a blender whirred furiously behind the counter. Wicked things are done to perfectly innocent booze in blenders. I didn't even have a chance to hurl myself on the Black & Decker to save my future hangover before she poured out something into a very tall glass and slid it across the bar.

It was brown. I had to give her that. So was the cafeteria floor over at Sundown Old Folks Casa on fajita and beans night. Whatever the brown goop was that she'd poured in the glass, it was thicker than oatmeal and stunk like compost.

I slid the glass back across the bar.

"My fault for not specifying that I like my booze sans mulch."

The stroke-victim smirk finally fled her face. "Booze? You mean like alcohol?" she asked, aghast.

"Booze, I mean like now."

"We don't serve alcohol here."

I left the dame passing judgment on me like I'd heckled the pope during Easter Mass and went back outside. I checked the sign. "The Seaweed Palace Bar."

I went back inside.

"You know, there are laws about truth in advertising, lady," I advised the dame at the bar. "My liver and I could make a citizen's arrest."

The offended barmaid was spared the full wrath of my nine hours of revolting sobriety by the annoyingly helpful voice that chose that moment to cut in behind me.

"This is a *health* bar, Mr. Banyon."

I turned. Another dame, another smile. At least this one didn't look like hers came from a prescription pad and a trip to the medical marijuana head shop.

"Kitten, if you don't know those two words are mutually exclusive, you're not doing either of them right. You Miss Ravioli?"

"Ravelli, yes," replied the woman my crackerjack office staff had spoken with on the phone. Chalk another one up for my dingbat secretary, who was probably running her mouth and her hair dryer at the same time she was writing down the client's name.

"I have a table out on the deck. Please, Mr. Banyon."

She had long blond hair, long tan legs, a short, gray business jacket and an even shorter skirt that hugged her can like a Campbell's soup label. She gestured, I walked.

The dame at the bar called out to the back of my departing trench coat. "I can whip you up today's special. Alfalfa and wheat curd frappe with lentils, and extra vitamin D."

"Tell you what," I called back to her. "I'll take this meeting first. That'll give you time to send out for another five of you, because one is nowhere near enough to pin me down and pour the goat's breakfast down my gullet."

Glass doors at the back of the evil joint with the lying name opened onto a wide wooden deck. There were a half-dozen round picnic tables, but no patrons. No big surprise there. The building was built directly on the shore, and waves rolled in and broke against the foundation. The deck extended out over the bay, and as I walked I looked down at the ominous dark water through the slats beneath my feet.

The table nearest the railing had on it a half-consumed glass of one of those sewage treatment-plant cocktails the dame out front tried to foist on me, plus a copy of the latest *Gazette* held in place by an unlit citronella candle.

My prospective client took the seat in front of her paper and glass of swill. I kept my Florsheims firmly planted on the deck.

"Sitting over water isn't the safest place to park your pretty little keister these days," I informed her. "And by yours, I mean mine."

"Mr. Banyon you do not know the half of it," she replied, with a weary sigh of authoritative certainty. But if Miss Ravelli knew so much about how dangerous the water had recently become she didn't show it as she calmly sucked down a lump of vitamin PDQ-enriched swamp juice and gestured for me to take a seat at the table.

I was tempted to tell her to take a long walk off a short pier, several of which were visible from where I was standing, but it had been weeks since my last paying client, and I was an ardent fan of pricey beverages that weren't cow-pat frappes in milkshake glasses.

I took the chair, but kept one eye patrolling the water for wayward tentacles. All I saw was one lonely fishing boat that had braved the deep and was at that moment chugging through the harbor with its morning haul, as well as one weirdo in a parka standing on the dock waiting for the ship to come in.

I didn't have a chance to ask Miss Ravelli what exactly it was she wanted from the thoroughgoing and courteous professionals of Banyon Investigations, before she dropped her newspaper in front of me.

"They shouldn't be allowed to print this trash," the dame complained.

"Let's speed this up, because at this moment the deeply concerned rats at the real bar where I should be getting drunk are forming a search party. Is there any trash in particular I'm supposed to be offended by, or is your beef with newspapers in general?"

She tapped a finger to the headline. **OCEAN'S ELEVEN!**

I'd already scanned the first few paragraphs of the article from a paper I'd swiped off a stoop that morning. It was the eleventh day of more of the same complaints from people who'd bought along the waterfront. Great real estate when you're splashing around with some beach bunnies having a ball in the summer sun; not so swell when your seafront cottage has been reduced to kindling by the latest storm surge.

"You owned one of those houses? Tough break. On the other hand, hordes of local artists with no talent can't keep up with collecting all the driftwood. You will be happy to know that your house will live on as scraps of busted-up wood painted with cartoon whales hanging by hunks of rope from the walls of moron tourists with no taste. So you see, God doesn't close a door without opening a window to jump out of. Hopefully you're high up enough that you don't survive the fall."

She tugged a dangling knot from her long yellow hair and offered a miserable sigh through perfect lips. "God is exactly why I want to hire you, Mr. Banyon."

I didn't like the way she said it, all knowing and mysterious. I'm a fan of smug like I'm deeply in love with sobriety, and if I want mystery I'll stick with Ellery Queen.

The mystery got a whole lot less mysterious the next second.

I'd kept an eye on the bay. The fishing boat had chugged up to a dock in one piece. It turned out the nut sweating in the parka was standing at a different pier. He had nothing to do with the fishermen. I barely noticed any of them, because at that moment something began to rise from the water's depths out in the middle of the bay.

"That's our cue to go, lady," I said, jumping up and tugging my trusty piece from its holster under my armpit.

I tried to get Miss Ravelli to get behind me but the dame just sat there like a bump on a log in a hole in the bottom of the sea. She was watching the water curve up like the tinfoil cap on a pan of Jiffy Pop, and as the waves broke around the rising object that was now heading right for us she clucked her tongue and checked her watch.

The dizzy broad who still hadn't gotten up from the picnic table was on her own.

For some guys there's a fine line between brave and stupid. For me there was about two city blocks, which was the location of the nearest train platform and which I figured I could cover at a sprint uninterrupted while my would-be client was thrashing around in the jaws of whatever glistening sea monster was about to drop in for lunch at the back of The Seaweed Palace Bar.

I'd backed up only one step when the first face broke the water.

Black eyes, long snout. The mouth ran back in a narrow trapdoor slit which was open wide and making happy little screeching noises as soon as it hit the air. It balanced a beach ball on the tip of its nose as it floored it toward the dock at the back of the bar.

I holstered my gun. Thanks to some do-gooder politicians with a fish fetish, there's a law in this state against shooting dolphins. I found that out the expensive way a few years back during an aquarium caper that ended with me and a school of killer mackerel handcuffed in the back of a paddy wagon. Don't ask.

The dolphin following the bouncing ball was just taking point. It was followed by four more, these ones yoked up in pairs. The reason why the annoying, playful bastards of the sea were harnessed together like carriage horses was clear the instant the item the five of them were dragging finally bobbed to the surface.

It was a pretty ordinary chariot. Bulky and gold and

worthless for pretty much anything other than showing off. The same applied to the pretty boy who held onto the reins with casual disinterest and allowed momentum to right the chariot.

It skimmed like a son of a bitch across the surface of the water.

There were more waves in the chariot owner's Farrah Fawcett hair than there were in the bay. He shook out his barely damp *Charlie's Angels* hair like a proud horse with a state fair blue ribbon pinned in its mane. His flowing hair was so yellow and blinding that I could have stuck him in the sky and given the sun the rest of the summer off.

The team of dolphins pulling the underwater chariot stopped at the deck behind the Seaweed Palace, and their boss stepped off with a confident glide before the coach even came to a complete stop. A short set of stairs extended to a slip behind the bar, and he bounded up two at a time. The deck swayed as he strode over to me, and when his shadow of doom fell over me I felt like an eyewitness on that airfield in New Jersey just before the Hindenburg went up like a birthday cake with gasoline frosting.

He was a good six feet, eight inches, but not pieced together in a lab like some gangly NBA player. This particular brick shithouse had the perfect, hulking proportions of a bronzed ape. His simple white shirt and pants were at least three sizes too small and threatened to pop every seam every time a muscle danced, which meant he probably spent a bundle on personal seamstresses because potato chip factories have fewer ripples. There were no shoes on his massive clodhopper feet, which I'm sure brought relief to a thousand Third World Avia child laborers slaving over vats of cheap, bubbling glue.

He first ran his fingers through his golden locks and only when he was finished grooming did a thumb like a canned ham with a fingerprint on it jerk in my direction.

"This him?" he snarled at Miss Ravelli.

I answered for her. "That depends on several variables, and I am unfortunately too sober at the moment to accurately run the numbers. So let's just keep it simple and say that I am definitely not him, I have no interest in being him, but if I see him I'll tell him you were looking for him."

The behemoth looked confused, which seemed a hell of a lot more comfortable on him than that shirt with the exploding buttons he was squeezed into.

"It's him," Miss Ravelli informed the hulking beach bum. "Crag Banyon, I'd like you to meet Poseidon, the god of the sea."

He had a grip like a dead uncle of mine who always tried to prove how tough he was by trying to break the bones in my six-year-old hand. Poseidon shook my hand all the way back over to the picnic table and shook me right back into the chair I'd just vacated.

"You tell him already?" Poseidon asked, dropping his massive bulk into the seat beside mine. Miss Ravelli shook her head.

"Save your breath," I told them. "I don't take god or ghost cases. If I ever make up a new business card, I'll have that printed above my name and telephone number. In fact, I'll have that printed up *instead* of my name and telephone number. Those two pains in the ass have always been more trouble than they're worth."

There was a crash, the deck shook underneath my pained ass, and all of a sudden I was staring close-up at one of Poseidon's massive feet.

"You see that?" the god of the sea demanded.

"I assume you don't mean that disturbing pedicure, your apparent spray tanning addiction or the fact that you shave your legs like a girl, and that you're calling my attention to the ankle monitor."

"Damn straight," Poseidon said, wiggling his toes.

The metal and plastic monitor was as big around as a toilet seat, yet was still pressed in tight against his skin. Two little lights, red and green, decorated the side nearest me. The red light was dead, but the green blinked.

"Honey," Miss Ravelli said quietly.

She touched the back of Poseidon's hand and only then did it seem to click for him that sticking a foot on someone's placemat might be okay for a Uruguayan rugby team and a zombie picnic but was not done in polite company, which she apparently mistakenly thought I was. He dropped the foot back to the deck and with the resulting thunder a few faces peeked out the back windows of the health bar to check for rain.

Poseidon crossed his massive arms over his barrel chest, sprang his last two buttons with his heavy sigh, and yielded the floor.

"Just give us one minute of your time, Mr. Banyon," Miss Ravelli said. "You came all the way down here, what's one more minute? We'll pay you."

She reached into her purse as she spoke and removed a single gold coin, which she slid past silent Poseidon and deposited next to one of the sea god's buttons which had rolled to a stop in front of me. It looked like an old Spanish doubloon, probably salvaged from some wreck on the ocean's floor. The dame was sending a message: there were plenty more sunken ships and tons more coins like that if I took the gig.

I slid the coin back her way, with Poseidon just sitting there between us like a waterlogged sumo watching the doubloon make the return trip.

"I don't have very many principles," I said, "which makes it real easy to keep track of the few I've got. First one: I don't bribe." (Sometimes I hate being such an upstanding son of a bitch.) "But if you want a shrink to unburden on, the train for downtown doesn't leave for another twenty minutes so you can have me another ten. After that I plan on being as drunk as fast as this city's fine public transit system permits."

Miss Ravelli took a deep breath and let it all out.

"Poseidon and I are married, although I mostly still use my maiden name. It makes it simpler for my charity work. You seemed not to know me which, Mr. Banyon, is actually a wonderful relief for a change. You see, I'm sort of a celebrity. I was a former Olympic swimmer. Silver medal in the Bongo Congo summer games. Should have been the gold, but that was the year the Russians entered that five thousand pound great white shark in a babushka in competition. I was one of only two swimmers that Olga Toothchenko didn't eat. They changed the rules about allowing marine predators to compete after that, but her record stands so it doesn't do me or No-Arms Sanchez any good. Flash forward six years. Poseidon and I met while I was swimming the English Channel to raise aware-ness for the Swimmer's Ear Foundation. I'm international spokesperson. I was swimming, he was diverting currents, and we fell in love. The wedding coverage was all over ET, GMA, all the light entertainment news shows, two years ago. It's so refreshing to meet someone who isn't into the whole celebrity thing."

Like everybody else who says they don't like the celebrity thing, it was the dame's lead story.

"My invitation must have got lost in the mail," I said.

"Is the lady boring you?" Poseidon demanded. Even seated he towered over me, and he made an extra effort to add a few inches with a suddenly rigid spine.

Self-preservation is an instinct deeply ingrained in the human animal. Unfortunately in me it's trumped by the dominant gene of being chronically annoyed with numskull deities who think they can push around everything that can't shoot lightning from its fingertips or knock up a goat.

"Yes, as a matter of fact, she is," I suicidally informed the god. "But I said I'd listen, so I am, and every interruption brings the one o'clock train closer."

Poseidon didn't seem to know what to do. As a god he was used to using only his impressive physique to bully around squid and starfish for millennia. Out of the ocean's depths he seemed out of his element and unsure what to do when the simple glare that always terrified whole schools of minnow no longer cut it. Lucky for me it didn't occur to him that he had mitts like snow shovels and could have taken my head like a sand dollar, crushed it to pennies and scattered the grains across the bay.

"Hon, it's okay," Miss Ravelli interjected, again with a delicate touch to the back of his massive hand. "Mr. Banyon is here to help."

"Let's set that falsehood aside for now," I suggested. "What else you got? Start with that." I aimed my chin to the floor where the ankle monitor softly beeped.

The sea god slumped back in his seat, and his wife

continued.

"It comes off next Monday," she said. "It's a whole big hullabaloo that happened long before he and I met. Poseidon has been restricted to the sea ever since the Titanic sank. The Leprechaun Mafia owned a significant share of White Star Lines, and they were out a bundle when that ship went down. They had a whole bunch of pots of gold in the hold and they thought Poseidon sank it to retrieve the coins once the ship reached the bottom. He does a lot of salvage work. The leprechauns were out for blood."

"Yeah, guess who took the fall?" Poseidon interjected. "Always Poseidon. Like I control ice. Yeah, it's water technically, but — duh? — look at it. It's frozen. Geesh. And I was all the way over in the Indian Ocean when it happened. I had a sawtooth eel and a couple of manta rays who backed me up."

"That's right, dear," Miss Ravelli said.

He was warming to his subject, killing too much time. The wife saw me cast a bored eye at her watch. I gave her an it's-your-dime shrug.

"I mean, it's the same with underwater earthquakes. Everyone yells at *me* when there's a tsunami, but — hello? — what do you think is *under* the water, *more* water? It's *land*, geniuses. There's giant plates shifting and volcanoes erupting all over the place. I don't control any of that, despite what they say about me banging the ground. So don't point your fingers at me if your island winds up underwater and your village gets swept away, take it up with Vulcan or my brother, Mr. Bigshot Zeus."

"*Yes, dear*," Miss Ravelli said.

She had repeated it three times while he was talking

and this last time she raised her voice loud enough that he finally heard her. The god fell silent and she soothed the behemoth by massaging the back of his huge paw.

"Poseidon has missed every assembly on Olympus for the past hundred years. The rest of them have been fine with that, but the seas have been woefully underrepresented there for an entire century. Now that the monitor is finally coming off and Poseidon will finally be able to return to dry land, we've been getting all kinds of threats. We think someone doesn't want him free and is trying to intimidate him."

"We think that, do we?" I said. "What I was thinking is that he's doing a pretty good job tricking the monitor right now. Not on land, still over water."

Miss Ravelli nodded. "That's why I asked you to meet us here instead of at your office. He's only allowed in water or over it. For instance, boats are fine but beaches are off limits, and so on. This deck is over the water, so the monitor doesn't go off. We couldn't go inside or it would."

"What would happen then?"

Poseidon morosely grabbed up his wife's glass of brown sludge, took a swig, made a sour face, then shoved it back in front of her. He licked swill off his gleaming white teeth and made a point of ignoring us as he stared into the bay.

Miss Ravelli raised both palms. "Poof is what would happen, Mr. Banyon. Even gods die. If Poseidon goes on land before next Monday, he's…finished."

"Well *he's* not finished because *he's* not going on land," Poseidon mocked. "I'm not an idiot, you know." He tried to fold his arms emphatically across his barrel chest but was so angry that he momentarily forgot how. He worked it out on the third attempt.

Miss Ravelli's lips thinned and her brow creased with silent worry.

"What kind of threats are you getting?" I asked.

"Strange calls in the middle of the night," she said. "They don't say anything, they just blow bubbles and then hang up. Then there's this."

She snapped open her purse and passed me a folded slip of paper.

It was an ad for sea monkeys from the back of a comic book. Everything in the ad's header except "Own a BOWL-FULL (sic) OF HAPPINESS!" had been covered up by a bunch of crooked letters that had been cut out from some-where else and glued to the ad. Obviously somebody watched too many TV cop shows. The assembled letters said, "YOUR NEXT." Crummy English aside, it was clearly a reference to the sea monkey family, and by exten-sion the Poseidons. The eyes of the bowlful of previously happy sea bastards were crossed out with large black ink X's. Red Crayola blood was dripping from cartoon wounds over all their bodies. Real nice. I love outsider art.

Back when I was with the cops I once worked what we at first thought was a runaway case. Some local wood-carver had chiseled himself a talking puppet that took off from his shop. Beats me why he made the thing. What the old pervert did with his wood was none of my business. Turns out the puppet had fallen under the influence of one of those talking crickets. You know the kind; always hanging around the stage doors of junior puppet shows, whispering into Punch and Judy's ears or tickling Elmo. It's a sick world. Eventually toothpicks and bags of sawdust were getting mailed back to the old woodcutter's shop every hour. The elderly perv was going nuts. He didn't have any dough to pay the six dollars ransom, and since the puppet wasn't a real boy we had to treat it as simple theft and malicious destruction of property. We eventually caught the cricket creep, but by the time we got to his nest all that was left was the puppet's nose. Last I heard, the old man had a nervous breakdown and was living inside a whale. The cricket bastard paid his fine and hopped out of court a free insect. Got stepped on by some fat lawyer on the sidewalk in front of the courthouse. Crushed his little top hat and everything. Justice under the heel of a wingtip. I'll take what I can get.

The point is, there's a lot sicker going on in the world than a simple doctored sea monkey ad from the back pages of a Little Lulu funnybook. I think the dame knew that, but I could see there was something else. What's more Miss Ravelli knew that I'd spotted the look of fearful hesitation on her face. She screwed up her courage.

"Last week someone left a sea horse head in our bed," she blurted.

"That was probably just a joke," Poseidon quickly interjected.

"*It was no joke*," she snapped. She closed her eyes and pressed the fingertips of one hand to the bridge of her nose. "I'm sorry, Mr. Banyon, but between all this, plus the octopus strike going into its third week and the whirl-pool next door running all hours of the day and night, I haven't been getting much sleep lately."

Despite myself, I felt bad for the dame. Hell, I even felt bad for her moose-of-the-sea husband, who didn't seem to have a clue how to comfort her and so just slouched there feeling sorry for the both of them. But rules are rules and when it came to getting mixed up with gods I was more atheistic than Christopher Hitchens and Karl Marx wrapped up in one, which they were after their zombies stumbled into that voodoo cursed particle accelerator last summer.

"You should go to the cops," I said.

"I've been to see them," she insisted. "The detective I spoke with about all this was as stupid and pigheaded a man as I've ever met. People like him are the reason why I left dry land and went to live in the sea. And you, of course, dear," she said to Poseidon.

"Huhn?" asked the genius lump of barefooted testosterone sitting beside her.

"Detective Dan Jenkins isn't the only cop in town," I informed her.

She seemed surprised. "How did you know it was him?"

"Because you pretty much just recited the first two lines of the eulogy I have written for him and tucked away in the back of my desk drawer behind a celebratory bottle of Jack Daniels for when that glorious day finally arrives," I said. "Look, the only thing I can tell you is that you probably don't have to worry. You've got until Monday with that thing on your ankle? My advice is forget whoever is hassling you and just wait it out. If you still want to make waves once it's off, follow up on that note glued to the ad. It came from a newspaper, not a magazine. The letters are dull, not glossy, and it looks like cheap paper. I'd even venture to say it came from here in town. That looks like the Gazette New Roman font the local rag uses in its masthead. As far as the decapitated sea horse, if someone managed to get inside your undersea palace to plant it, question the help. That includes staff you think you can trust. Hell, I'll throw the two of you in there as suspects, since I have no idea what your motives might be vis-à-vis one another." I heard the whistle of an approaching train, and I stood. "And that, Mr. and Mrs. God of the Seven Deadly Seas is the mating call of my worried bartender who is praying that my wallet hasn't stumbled into a more reputable saloon and discovered the existence of clean floors and non-watery cocktails at surprisingly affordable prices."

Poseidon didn't even look at me. The wife's face was the very picture of grim acceptance as I turned to go.

A single pivot on one heel and I was turned right back in their direction.

"On the other hand, a thousand bucks if I catch your guy in the next five minutes," I announced.

They both glanced up at me. Or, rather, she did. Still hunched in his seat, Poseidon and I were finally eye to eye. Tan lids narrowed over blue orbs.

"What?" the pair of them asked in unison.

"Time's a-wastin'," I said, snapping my fingers to hustle business along. "A thousand bucks if I have your guy in hand in five minutes. American. I don't deal in doubloons or fish heads. Convert whatever currency you've got at the local bank. Deal?"

The wife quickly answered yes, and as reluctant as he was to trust anyone with a mortal lifespan and an IQ higher than the shallow end of the kiddie pool, the big, dumb sea god joined the party a split-second after his old lady's okay.

I strode past them over to the stairs Poseidon had taken up from the water. I took the steps at a trot and spun around to the dock that cut across the rear deck of the health bar. The dolphins acked up a storm as I hustled past them, and above me Poseidon and his wife watched as I hustled past their ankles toward the cluster of docks that were packed into the far end of the bay.

The crew of the fishing boat was nowhere to be seen. I heard some voices from the belly of their ship, and a remote-operated crane swung seemingly of its own volition on the main deck. There was only one person left out in the open in the whole area.

My back had been to him, and he'd been standing to Miss Ravelli's left and probably out of her line of site. The only one of our party who'd had a full-on, panoramic, 3D view of the silent spectator throughout our entire meeting was Poseidon, and the sea god had paid as much attention to him as gods do pretty much anything ranked below nymph on the Cambridge U. Scale of bangable supernatural creatures.

The guy I'd seen earlier still stood on the dock in his parka. I'd figured before that the coat was an odd choice for June, but it was cool near the shore thanks to the crazy ocean weather and the overcast day. Plus what do I know from fashion? Parkas in summer might've replaced crotches pulled down to the knees and underwear hanging out with the trendy moron set. I hadn't given the guy a second thought.

The bottom of the parka was fringed with some kind of dark, shredded material that I couldn't quite make out from a distance. A pair of spindly, tan legs ran from the weird fringe of the parka to a pair of cheap Wal-Mart flip-flops.

The coat's hood was up, and within the circle of white

fringe a pair of dark sunglasses stared out like a couple of beady bug's eyes.

Any moron would have seen that he was trying to get Poseidon's attention. Any moron, that is, save the moron whose attention he'd been trying to get.

Two steps brought me up to the pier on which the stranger loitered, and his head snapped around when he saw me heading straight for him.

"Okay, pal, let's you and me have a little thousand buck chat, shall we?" I called.

"Him," the Parka Man grunted, frantically shaking his head inside his fringed hood and pointing behind me to the godly lummox on the deck. "Him. Me want *him*."

"Hey, buddy, I want a tropical island retirement hut parked smack-dab on the same beach where the native babes wash their grass unmentionables, and a thousand smackers will buy me a real good set of dirty old man binoculars."

Beats me what was eating the guy, but something I said seemed to rattle his cage. Or maybe he just hated the sound of my voice, which put him in the same company as my ex-wife who listed that as number twenty-eight in the enumerated grounds on her divorce petition, right between not fixing the bathroom grout for six years (#27) and selling her deadbeat old man to Eskimos (#29). I'd've fixed this parka jerk up with the former Mrs. Banyon when this was all through, if only I thought the guy deserved to be banished to a hell of tossed frying pans, burned grilled cheese sandwiches and months of unwashed socks…a land where love and hope stuffed the tailpipe with a rag of grimy dreams and sat on the front seat together in the locked garage with the engine running.

Turns out a second later Parka Man gave me every reason in the world to give him my ex-wife's number, hire a minister, rent a hall and yank the pin on the bliss grenade.

The guy was smooth for a tourist. He pulled the rod on me before I even had a chance to grab under my coat for my roscoe. Lucky for me, his rod was an actual rod.

The metal bar was about three feet long and shiny. Could have been bronze; more likely gold. If he thought he'd whack me with it, that might've worked if his arms weren't quite so stubby and if I wasn't still over a hundred feet away.

The weirdo in the parka didn't aim the rod at me. He pointed it in the direction of the bay, and it was only then that I got a good look at the thing's headpiece. It had three fat prongs, the two outside ones curving out in either direction. There was some kind of flippered snake coiled around the base that clamped the prongs to the pole.

I already guessed what I was dealing with even before I heard the deep voice from the deck of The Seaweed Palace Bar at my back.

"Oh, bulfinch," Poseidon, the bastard god of the sea, swore.

I dug under my coat as I ran, and my hand was already wrapped around the butt of my piece, but it was already way too late.

The stranger in the parka swept his arm up and around in a broad arc, and brought it sharply down, the pointed tips aimed directly at me. Simultaneous with the gesture, a curl of water had risen up from the bay like a soggy question mark, and on the downward snap of his wrist it burst forward.

The stream of water roared at me like a cannonball blasted out of a bidet. It struck me full force in the chest and I went back into the granite foundation of the taffy shop next door to the health bar. I swore I heard a crack when my elbow whacked the wall, but then the back of my head slammed rock and there was nothing but a bright flash of stars.

I woke up seconds later on my hands and knees spitting water like a cheap Home Depot backyard fountain and listening to the percussion section of an all-horse marching band galloping John Philip Sousa's greatest hits from one side of my skull to the other.

Over the equine racket playing between my ears, I heard another sound.

The whine of a small motor assaulted my ringing ears, and I looked up to see the guy in the parka sitting in a little boat and already halfway to the other side of the bay.

He wasn't heading out to sea. This end of the bay angled in to the rear of a shopping mall that was built on a short cliff. There were small trees that had sprung up like weeds and partially obscured the J.C. Penney's and Gap signs on the rear loading dock side of the mall. The guy in the boat was heading for the stairs that led to the mall.

I pulled out my gun and squeezed off one shot. The slug dinged off the outboard motor. It coughed, spluttered to a stop and began to send out a cloud of thick black smoke, but by then the boat was already gliding up to the dock on the far side of the bay.

My attacker hopped from the little motorboat, out onto the dock and raced up the long staircase to the rear of the mall. He disappeared around the corner Footlocker.

I stood on the opposite side of the bay, panting, drenched, aching and with a pounding headache. It was pretty much how I felt on my most awful Sunday mornings, but without the pleasant lengthy numbness of the preceding Saturday night's debauchery.

Up on the deck of the health bar, Poseidon and Miss Ravelli held onto the railing and stared dumbly across the bay at the spot where Parka Man vanished.

"Yeah, I'm just fine, thanks for worrying," I snapped.

I fished angrily around in my trench coat pocket where I thought I'd felt a spare slug the other week. It had fallen through a hole and got stuck in the lining. I managed to pop it out and shove it into my piece before jamming the gun back in my holster.

I snatched my fedora from the dock. It had come through the attack relatively unscathed. I bent the damp brim back into shape and dropped it on my aching skull.

"Why didn't you tell me somebody stole your trident?" I demanded as I squished my way back across the wooden walkway.

Everybody knew that Poseidon's trident was like the atom bomb of the undersea world. Three prongs of heavy duty firepower that could be used to stop that pesky drip in the bathroom sink or summon tidal waves. I suddenly realized why the ocean had been so tumultuous lately. Poseidon's trident had fallen into the hands of some demented, bowlegged loon with a Nanook of the North fixation, and the first couple of the Mid-Atlantic Ridge hadn't bothered to tell the cops someone had looted the sea god's gun cabinet.

The pair of them exchanged a nervous glance. It was Miss Ravelli, of course, who was silently voted spokesman.

"We weren't sure it was stolen," she said. "Poseidon misplaces it sometimes, but it always turns up. You know how it is. You put down the car keys and you've searched the whole house three times and you're sure they're lost, then they suddenly turn up on the hook near the door where they were supposed to be all along. Last time the trident went missing I found it in the kitchen cupboard with the mops."

I squished back up the stairs to the deck. "I still want my thousand."

For *that* Poseidon found his voice. "You didn't catch him," he snarled.

"I was not in full possession of the facts," I said, more calmly than I felt. "Facts which, since they were not disclosed to me, nearly goddamn killed me while the two of you stood there and watched." I closed my eyes for a second and dripped on the deck. "Forget the thousand. I'll settle for a couple of aspirin." I waved a hand at her purse, which doubled as a pharmacy for every dame on the planet. Water ran from the sleeve of my trench coat and dribbled out onto the table.

"I don't believe in them," she apologized. "I only trust natural cures."

"Natural. Right. Dissolve two crystals under your tongue, and if that doesn't cure your migraine chop your head off. Goddamn new agers."

"You need not be so testy, Mr. Banyon," Miss Ravelli said. "My husband wanted to help, but if you must know *I* stopped him. The trident is a formidable weapon, but I saw that man was heading for shore. Poseidon couldn't go on shore with his ankle monitor, we explained that to you. We told you everything that we knew for certain."

"I'll be sure to explain all about your forthrightness to my concussion if it ever regains consciousness," I said. I started to go, but stopped dead. "You know, I get that you're afraid to make landfall and that by the time you saddled up and took off after him, he'd probably have been over the other side. Gutless, girly, and ungodlike, but I get it. But why didn't you just send the damn dolphins to cut him off?"

"I'm not Aquaman, for Christ's sake," Poseidon snapped. "I can't just—"

He pressed his fingers to his temple and bugged his eyes in a sarcastic pantomime of shooting out telepathic rays.

His team of dolphins instantly took off from the dock below the bar and raced across the bay to the spot where Parka Man had jumped to the dock. They splashed around doing those annoying ack-ack dolphin noises, swimming in circles offshore.

"What the hell?" Poseidon said. "I didn't know I could do that. Damn."

"It's all right, darling," Miss Ravelli cooed. She rubbed her delicate little mortal hand on the back of Poseidon's clumsy catcher's mitt.

That's how I left them. Her rubbing his massive mitt and cooing soothing and sweet you're-not-stupids in his ear, and him literally scratching his peroxide blond head and trying to figure out how to get his team of runaway dolphins to make the return trip across the bay.

The dame behind the counter flashed her idiot's grin

as I marched through the main bar. "Are you sure I can't get you something, sir?" she asked.

"No," I snapped, and immediately changed my mind. "Yes. A towel, some aspirin and a bottle of water."

I was surprised when she managed to produce all three. The aspirin she collected from her own purse, which she stuffed quickly back below the bar, making sure that none of her hippie-dippy coworkers had seen the Anacin label.

I threw back the pills, drank as little of the Poland Springs as possible (water is for bathing, flushing, or freezing into cubes), and wrapped the towel around my neck.

"Thanks," I said, handing back the water bottle. "Recycle that into swizzle sticks. And send the bill to the barefoot behemoth making wolf whistles at the school of dolphins from the back porch."

When I got back outside I heard the sound of the one o'clock train rumbling away from the platform two blocks away. The next one wasn't due for another forty-five minutes. It'd be quicker to hike all the way back to the office.

"Monotheism didn't put all you Olympus bastards out of business fast enough," I grumbled. A garden gnome exiting the taffy shop next-door overheard me and shot me a look like I was the one wearing the pointed hat and ceramic lederhosen. I resisted the urge to make a field goal with the little son of a bitch between a pair of telephone poles.

Leaving a dripping trail down the sidewalk, I trudged back toward the shriveled black heart of the decaying city.

2

The six story sandstone slouched in the middle of the block like a killer who'd volunteered for the search party but was trying to go unnoticed in the crowd.

The building was a dump but the rent was cheap, which was the primary reason it was the international home of that indispensable Western institution, Banyon Investigations, Inc. I saw from the sidewalk as I approached that the name on the third floor window was barely visible, and looked more like "Banjo Invest.....Inc."

I'd planned to get it repainted months ago, but some jerks had recently begun wandering in off the street asking me for stock recommendations. I'd been telling them all to buy IBM and pocketing the fifty bucks advice fee. Hey, you wander blind into some lousy joint in a crummy neighborhood asking a guy named Banjo who looks shifty like me where you should shovel your money, you get what you pay for. Besides, I'd been checking lately and since I started my inadvertent side business IBM had been going through the roof. That was the main reason I'd filched a paper on the way to my meeting with Mr. and Mrs. Poseidon. If I'd only taken the loot I'd made and followed my own advice instead of blowing it at local taverns I'd be sitting pretty.

The street outside the building was packed tighter than Zombie Liberace's colon.

Thanks to the craziness going on out at sea, most fishermen were too scared to go networking. Consequently, fish for sale was growing scarce and prices were soaring. The only place in town not negatively impacted by the shortage was the dingy fish market that stunk up most of the ground floor of my building.

Business was booming at For the Halibut Fish Bazaar. The owner, Luigi Vincetti, had even used some of the proceeds to fix his ice machine, which had broken during the Johnson administration and which he'd subsequently used as a playpen for his moron sons when they were snot-nosed little brats. The Vincetti spawn were long grown, but from the stench I always figured the sentimental old dago had stored all their diapers in the beat-up old ice maker. Cheaper than tipping the garbage man at Christmas.

Vincetti's place hadn't been negatively impacted by the lack of fresh fish in the local marketplace mainly because "fresh" was not a word in the Vincetti pidgin lexicon. All the healthy eaters in town were flocking to For the Halibut, without a clue that it was the last stop on the town's ptomaine tour.

There were cars double parked on both sides of the street, a meter maid gleefully tearing pages from her ticket book like my ex-wife writes checks, and emaciated health fanatics in Lycra bike pants crowding every inch of the sidewalk.

On my way in through the building's side door I saw the counter dame from The Seaweed Palace Bar entering

Vincetti's place along with a crush of customers. She wasn't half bad on the eyes, and if I knew she was going my way I would've asked her out and awarded her the privilege of driving me across town.. As it was, she'd probably fall for the doctor who'd be pumping her stomach by sundown. Story of my life.

At least the elevator wasn't crowded. For some reason it was the only spot in the whole building that was air conditioned, which was true winter as well as summer, and the clothes I thought had mostly dried on my long walk felt wetter than ever in the cold.

The upstairs hallway was quiet for a change. Myron Wasserbaum, the bastard dentist down the hall, had organized all the cases against him into a single class action and was spending Thursdays these days at the courthouse staring into the toothless maws of his victims, so the scream machine in his office was off that afternoon.

Madame Carpathia's Dance Studio on the top floor had been shut down for the past week. Some ballerina had started a gang war when she wore a pair of stolen slippers to class. Turns out she'd dropped a Winnebago on some witch over in the barrio and stole her shoes, and all hell broke loose when senora's sister showed up at Madame Carpathia's to claim her dead hermana's zapatos. Twenty years ago they were shooting each other over Air Jordans, now they're launching fireballs and tossing pails of water over some ruby red slippers. The whole world is going to hell.

My own office at the end of the hall was quiet as well. I was happy to see there wasn't anybody waiting for me when I stepped inside. I'd had it up to here with clients and didn't care if another one didn't darken my door for another six months.

My secretary wasn't at her desk in the outer office.
Doris was in the hospital getting her tonsils out and needed
a few days off. When she told me that morning the reason
she needed time off I admitted I was surprised.

"Why?" Doris accused, planting her hands on her hips
and snapping her gum so viciously I knew that she was
imagining my mug on the popping pink Bazooka bubble.
"It ain't so strange, people get their tonsils out all the
time."

"I just assumed, Doris, that a woman who spends so
much of her day yapping on the phone would have worn
her tonsils down to insignificant nubs by this late stage in
life." It was my smile that got a high heel heaved at my
head.

"You're a bastard, Crag Banyon."

She didn't speak to me again the rest of the morning
except to scream at me the wrong name of the client who'd
called for a meeting at the bayside health bar.

The elf holding down the fort behind my dingbat
secretary's desk looked up with a pair of tennis ball eyes
when I walked through the door. His face brightened when
he saw it was me.

"Hello, Mr. Crag," Mannix, my office assistant and
all-around go-to gofer sang happily. "You had one phone
call."

"Court, cops, collection agency, or the former Mrs.
Banyon?" I asked as I walked straight past him and through
the door to my private office.

"None of those people," the elf said. He scooped up
a scrap of paper from Doris' desk and hustled to keep up
with me. "It was from Miss Ravelli. She said she was the

woman who you met with today, but I checked the file and Miss Doris had written that person's name down as 'Ravioli.' Should I start a new file?"

"Yeah," I said, tossing the towel I'd carted clear across town to my beat-up couch and stripping off my hat, coat and suit jacket. "Write on the tab 'Replacement Secretary Front Runners,' then run over to St. Attila's Home of Criminally Psychotic Females and get a list of their twenty most likely recidivist recent parolees, including most violent offenses, body count and weapons of choice. Then leave that file in Doris' top drawer. You got all that? Good."

Mannix stood there holding the scrap of paper in his hand, unsure what to do with it. His big eyes watched in confusion as I climbed out onto the fire escape and hung my suit coat and trench coat in the sun on the rusty railing. He was still standing mute in front of my desk when I climbed back inside.

"What did she say, Mannix?" I asked wearily as I sat my fedora on the windowsill and draped my tie next to it.

"Oh," said the elf. He glanced at his note. "Miss Ravelli said she was sorry for what happened and that she and her husband would still like to hire you to find the item. That's exactly what she said, Mr. Crag. 'The item.' She wouldn't tell me what the item is. Is it candy?" When those huge eyes looked up they'd developed a hopeful glint.

"Not with that health nut," I said. "Is that all she had to say?"

"She left her number," Mannix said.

"Oh, I *got* that dame's number," I said. "Stick that note in the Ravioli file and dump it down the incinerator."

Mannix went back out into the outer office and a moment later I heard a file cabinet drawer roll open and slide shut.

I wasn't sure if he thought I was serious about St. Attila's. Mannix was an ex-Christmas elf who'd worked the North Pole factories for over a hundred years. If anybody did sarcasm up there they didn't do it very well, and Mannix had a hard time recognizing it. I would have set the kid straight about the joke, but part of me hoped that he'd do as I said and leave that folder for Doris. I wondered how loud she'd be able to scream at me with the holes where her tonsils used to be packed in rocky road ice cream.

I changed into a spare white dress shirt from my closet and returned to my desk.

There was still a crowd down in the street. The meter maid had summoned a couple of tow trucks, and they were in the process of hauling away two of the double parked cars. Some of the others had been booted and would sit out in the street blocking in the cars that were legally parked, forcing their owners to feed money in the meters across the street for vehicles that couldn't be moved. Government. A nice little racket to get into. Too bad the assholes who manage it own the monopoly.

Vincetti was down there by then. I could see him waving his arms and hollering at the meter maid for chasing away the only business he'd had in years. It was the same frantic choreography he usually reserved for chasing off his more everyday clientele, the army of stray cats that regularly camped out front waiting in vain for the old fishmonger to throw out so much as one moldy sardine.

I was turning away from the window when I caught a glimpse of something white and furry on the sidewalk across the street.

It wasn't like he went out of his way to make himself hard to spot in a crowd. The fringe of his hood was aimed up toward my window, and I got a good look at that familiar pair of glinting bastard sunglasses plus a streak of white sunscreen greasing up the tip of a broad nose. The glasses weren't the only thing glinting.

Poseidon's trident was already up and aimed my way.

The meter maid didn't notice. Vincetti wouldn't have cared if he had. Everybody else walked by without giving a second glance to the most powerful weapon in the maritime world in the tan hand of a little maniac wearing a pair of cheap public shower slippers and no pants.

I heard a vicious gurgle in the corner of my office from the direction of my water cooler, and I was flinging myself to my stomach even as I hollered out the open door.

"Hit the dirt, Mannix!"

I landed hard on the elbow I'd already smashed an hour before and curled up in a ball in the dark footwell of my desk.

There was a crunch across the room like someone stomping on a hundred boxes of peanut brittle at once, and I knew from the million tiny shards of plastic that harpooned the thin front of my desk that the water cooler had just exploded.

The room rattled, my desk was shoved back, and my lamp thudded somewhere unseen. Water splashed across the floor. The cuff of one shirt sleeve was instantly soaked and I got dotted by the backsplash from the cascade of water that splattered the wall and window behind my desk. It was over in about three seconds.

I sat there bravely cowering for over a minute, but the

second assault never came.

As I climbed back out I heard some fabric tear and only then did I notice that one of the bits of hard plastic that had speared my desk had gone through my clean shirt. My upper arm was bleeding like a son of a bitch and, worse, when I stood I saw that the precious grime I'd spent years cultivating was running down the wall and window in muddy rivulets. In one stroke of aquatic vandalism, the parka bastard had robbed my office of an entire decade's worth of grubby P.I. atmosphere.

"You all right, Mannix?" I called.

The elf poked his head in my office, the very picture of perfect health. He surveyed the water cooler, which lay in burst-open ruins in the corner, and the front of my desk which looked like it had suffered a frontal assault from a plastic porcupine.

"Can I go home for the day?" he asked.

"No," I said. "And stop talking to Doris. She's a rotten influence on you."

I looked out the window. Parka Man was nowhere to be seen.

I climbed out the window and clanked double-time down the rusty stairs. The retractable ladder to my sandstone deathtrap was locked solid so I had to hang from the second floor landing of the fire escape and drop to the sidewalk. I pushed through the crush of people, nearly got plowed over by a city garbage truck that I figured was making a delivery to Vincetti's, and somehow made it to the opposite side of the street in one stumbling piece.

I looked around, but there was no one nearby to interview. The meter maid was yelling into her radio for backup to come collect one furious fishmonger, and Vincetti was puffing his elderly way back across the street to barricade himself inside his market. His replay of the Siege of Florence would have worked better if he hadn't had all the fish inside laminated. Even the local cops weren't dumb enough to let him send out for pizza.

I glanced around the ground where Parka Man had been standing but the only thing that looked out of place was a single, very long strand of some kind of dried weed.

I grabbed up the flora and headed back across the street. This time it was a laundry truck that nearly creamed me, and I barely avoided the speeding bumper with a complicated little double-yellow-line dance step that would have made Madame Carpathia proud. I landed backwards on the sidewalk with my heels teetering on the curb, did another pirouette, regained my confident footing with the grace of Gene Kelly, and proceeded to plow straight into the counter dame from The Seaweed Palace Bar.

Girl, her pocketbook contents, and smelly Vincetti fish went everywhere.

"Sorry, babe," I said. "But in my defense you're a crummy defensive walker."

I pocketed the hunk of weed I'd found on the sidewalk across the street and gallantly pulled her up off her ass. I'm a regular Sir Walter Raleigh.

The dame scowled at me and went to work scooping everything back into her handbag, including the bottle of aspirin that was two pills lighter thanks to yours truly. The last thing she grabbed up from the sidewalk was her package of rotten wrapped fish, and she carefully examined the paper for tears.

"Yeah, it's important none of Vincetti's fresh fish

escapes its wrappers. Last time the EPA had the block quarantined for a month. He's not quite reached Chernobyl level yet, but I hear he's cultivating some salmon in the back room that should give the Reds a run for their rubles in a few years in the ecological Armageddon department. We didn't meet properly back at that fruitcake factory you call a job. Name's Banyon."

Just five minutes since being nearly murdered for the second time that day, yet still smooth as a Burma-Shave kisser. I could give Zombie Hefner lessons.

"I know who you are," she snapped. "You owe me for that towel and the bottled water. Those people you told me to bill wouldn't pay, and it's coming out of my salary."

"Of course they wouldn't," I said, shaking my head. "Why would the richest couple on the Forbes 500 Deep Sea Edition shell out for the cost of a towel for the guy they almost got murdered? It's just lucky for all of us they evidently told you who I was so we could make sure the right sap got the bill."

It turned out Mannix wasn't the only one who didn't do sarcasm.

"Absolutely," she agreed. "Those bottled waters are four bucks each. Anyway, it's lucky for you they told me your name so I knew it when your friend came in looking for you just after those two left. Did he find you?"

"My friend," I said, already knowing where this was heading. "He about this tall, with a pair of General Mac-Arthur sunglasses and Admiral Peary's windbreaker?"

"That's him," she said. "He asked your name, and I'd just found out from them, so I told him and I said you'd just headed down the sidewalk. It couldn't have been more than a couple of minutes after you left. You mean he didn't catch up with you?"

It wasn't the least bit peculiar to the dim bulb that the good friend that she'd set on my trail hadn't known my name. I wondered if Doris had kept from me the fact that she'd had a long-lost sister matriculating in a petri dish at Harvard all these years.

"Oh, dear," the dingbat counter girl complained. She tried to brush away some thick sidewalk grime she'd just noticed on her skirt but only smeared it worse. She tsked and tried to wipe the gunk off her palm, succeeding only in smearing both palms black. She looked up in desperation. "What are you even doing here?" she accused.

"My office," I explained. "Upstairs." I pointed up to the third story window, outside of which the arms of my trench coat were flapping hello from the fire escape.

"Banjo Invest?" she said. "The financial councilor? My roommate lost three thousand bucks last week following your advice. She had to quit her job and move back to Wichita to live with her parents. Now I'm stuck with her share of the rent."

"It's more art than science," I admitted. "You want to buy me dinner?"

She threw her fish at my head and stormed off down the street.

A cruiser had drawn up the block and the patrolman was conferring with the meter maid. I could see Vincetti's frightened, beady peepers peering through the eyes of the cartoon lobster that was painted on his window.

I framed my mouth with both hands and hollered through the makeshift megaphone to the cops across the street. "He says he hates cops for framing Sacco and

Vanzetti and he wants the same funeral director the Mussolini family uses!"

Vincetti's eyes popped wider than the cartoon lobster's and he ran screaming from the window. More cop cars were swarming up both ends of the street as I hastily reentered my end of the building. I didn't want to be in the line of fire when they started reenacting the toll booth scene from *The Godfather* with old Vincetti as Sonny stumbling around the street with a .45 caliber flounder dangling from his fingers.

Upstairs, Mannix had found a pair of pliers and was pulling plastic water cooler shards from the front of my desk.

My office looked like a dusty car after a rainstorm. Until ten minutes before you could have written "wash me" in the dust on the walls. Now the streaks of mud running from where my precious dry dust had been made it look like some graffiti bastard had gone nuts all around the room with a Hershey's squirt bottle.

I snatched up my lamp, which was wedged between the wall and a file cabinet, and slammed it back onto my desk. I felt two simultaneous pains, the first from my elbow which was having the worst day of its life, the second from my bicep.

Turns out the tear in my shirt and the bleeding from my upper arm was from more than the one shard of plastic that had jabbed me while I was heroically hiding out under my desk. Another, smaller piece had apparently gone straight through the front desk panel and was still sticking in my arm. In all the fun and near-death of the previous five minutes, I hadn't even noticed.

"Dammit," I groused, pulling the plastic chunk out. It

was as small as a toothpick, but sharp as hell. I dropped it to my damp blotter. "Get the first aid kit, Mannix."

The elf hustled over to my closet and returned with a white tin box with a red cross on it. The kit used to be loaded up with Band-Aids, hydrogen peroxide and all the usual useless medicinal bullshit, but I'd made sure that they'd all been crowded out by one large bottle of the most important medicine on earth.

I poured myself a couple of belts of Seagram's, downing them one after the other until the multiple pains in my arm became less important than the pain in the ass who was responsible for them. I slammed down my glass onto my damp blotter, getting doubly angry when the cloud of dust that usually exploded from the surface of my desk with such dramatic displays failed to materialize.

"Mannix," I called to the elf who'd slipped back into the other office. "Get Miss Ravioli on the phone."

3

"I'm sorry that you had a problem at your office, Mr. Banyon, but I can't see what it has to do with me or my husband."

The god of the sea's wife was playing it cooler than the lead beatnik in a bongo quartet. At first she didn't answer her cell phone herself. She let me pass up three layers of servants before she deigned to come on the line. She was in full politician spin mode before she even opened her mouth, denying and obfuscating like an amateur magician tossing a blanket over the two boxes he's just sawed in half and trying to cover for all the blood all over the stage with a lousy card trick.

"I don't even know who that man was," Miss Ravelli said. "Poseidon and I never saw him before in our lives. You were the one who pointed him out to us. You were the one he attacked then ran from. Maybe he's someone with a grudge against you."

"I've got an entire phone book of people with grudges against me, sister, and not one of them has a magic pitchfork that controls water."

"Well... I still don't know," she said.

"Look, I don't know either. I don't know, for instance,

what you've got me mixed up in, but whoever this maniac is he followed me because he obviously thinks I'm working for you. Therefore, I want you to let everybody under the sun and sea know I'm not in it and I never was. Take out a full-page ad in the *New York Times*, hire skywriters. Hell, send an owl to the goddamn Ministry of Magic if that's what it takes."

"Oh, now *that's* just silly," she said. "I don't know what kind of fantasy world you live in, Mr. Banyon, but my husband Poseidon — the god of the sea who rules from a barnacle-encrusted gilded marble palace at the bottom of the ocean — and I live in the real world. Now, we would be more than happy to hire you for that matter we discussed. Have you changed your mind?"

"I almost had it lobotomized by a chunk of exploding water cooler, but luckily it's the same one, so it's still not stupid enough to get within twenty thousand leagues of whatever it is you people are tied up in."

"In that case, Mr. Banyon, we have nothing further to discuss."

She broke the connection before I could thank her for not picking up the check for one measly towel and a bottle of water.

Mannix had already collected all the broken shards of plastic from around the office and swept them into a Glad bag. He'd wheeled out the remains of the cooler and was just reentering the room when I slammed down the desk phone.

"Is something wrong, Mr. Crag?" the elf asked.

"I am the magnet of wrong, Mannix. I am the epicenter of wrong. I am the sun at the center of the goddamn solar system of wrong, around which all the planets of wrong rotate on a daily basis to shower shit on. There is *always* something wrong, Mannix. I just wish for once in my life it'd be wrong somewhere on the other side of town."

I leaned back and grabbed my tie off the windowsill. It was made from the same space-age material as Frisbees, so it was already dry. I looped it contemplatively around my neck and wondered how tight I'd have to pull it to end my misery.

On the street down below a heavily armed SWAT team was leading old Vincetti into the back of a police van. He was yelling in Italian and trying to call the cops' attention to me waving down at him from my office window.

"I guess there's always a bright side," I said. I leaned out the window and hauled my suit jacket and trench coat in from the fire escape.

Pretty much everything was pretty much dry. I heaved on my rumpled layers, snatched up my hat and headed for the door. I'd nearly made it, but at the last second I grabbed the door frame and leaned back into the room.

"Mannix, do me a favor and dig up whatever you can find on this Ravelli dame," I said reluctantly.

"Yes, sir, Mr. Crag. Are we taking the case?"

"No. Definitely, unequivocally no. But if I'm going to get killed for no good reason, I want to know exactly who I'm libeling in my obituary."

I departed the Banyon Investigations suite and headed straight for the elevator. I'd tapped the down button and was cooling my heels in front of the closed silver door when there was a sudden flash at the end of the hall, like one of those courthouse steps scenes in old movies where the press lights up a hundred flashbulbs all at once.

A gust of gale force wind burst down the hall and I

was suddenly holding onto the elevator doorframe for dear life. Beats me where my hat blew off to, because at that moment I was too blinded by the blast of light to see around the dancing black spots. A crack of simultaneous thunder rattled my eardrums

As quick as the storm struck, it passed. The wind died, my coat stopped flapping like a flag up a pole and my eyes cleared well enough to see the naked guy standing down the hallway in front of the closed door to my offices.

He was built like one of those Hollywood jerks who spend more time at the gym than the library but are still experts on all the nuances of everything they don't read about.

He wasn't completely naked. A little towel wrapped his waist so, provided he didn't bend over to pick something up off the floor, my world was safe. He wore a little pair of felt booties that would have shamed Errol Flynn and a hat that looked like a satin construction helmet that had been shrunk in the wash. Tiny little wings adorned both shoes and hat, yet I doubted he was there to make a Church's Chicken delivery.

The SOB had immortal deity written all over him, and unless I missed my guess I was looking at Mercury, the messenger god and patron saint of UPS, FedEx, and all those crooked US Postal workers who suddenly get religion when they finally get caught with forty years of undelivered mail stuffed out in the garage.

My shit luck, the god saw me cooling my heels by the elevator.

"Hey, you. Mortal," Mercury demanded. "You Banyon?"

I made a show of looking behind me, then pointed a

confused finger at myself. (My improvisational skills are the envy of that whole asshole Groundlings crowd.)

"Me? Banyon? I wish," I said. I found my fedora and grabbed it up, talking as I marched right towards him. "Unfortunately, I'm Myron Wasserbaum, D.D.S., the worst dentist in the twelve boroughs, and that includes the one over in Dickery who was feeling up all his patients in the chair. I can supply you with all your dental needs, provided you need the wrong tooth pulled or your brand-new fillings to drop out next week."

"I am a god, mortal. We have no need for dentists."

"That's good for you, because spit gives me hives and I faint at the sight of incisors." I cut short before I reached him, slapping open the door to the stairwell. "Remember, that's Myron Wasserbaum. Be sure to tell all your friends how rotten I am."

Mercury's eyes narrowed as he looked past me. He was reading something, and as he did so he raised a curious brow. "Isn't that your office down there?"

"Yes, it is. However, I just remembered I forgot to get drunk this morning."

At least that part was mostly true.

The last I saw of the messenger god, he and his winged moccasins were walking past the blown-apart water cooler Mannix had left in the hallway and striding through my office door. My pal the elf was unfailingly honest, so that didn't leave me much time.

I took the stairs at a sprint and for good measure took the back door to the alley and hustled over to the next block.

I wouldn't have thought after the hilarious exploding water cooler gag that I could possibly hate Poseidon and his Olympic swimmer wife even more.

As far as I knew, Mercury only brought messages from other gods. Which meant either Poseidon himself was sending me a love letter behind the little woman's back or another Olympian had been dragged into my wake thanks to the two of them.

As I hustled along the afternoon streets, I kept a watchful eye out to make sure my newly acquired and rapidly expanding fan club wasn't tagging along behind me.

It's hard enough to lose a tail when you know you've got one, it's doubly hard when you've got to keep an eye trained on every puddle to make sure it doesn't magically leap up and go for your jugular while simultaneously watching the skies for golden chariots to hurl out of the sun and cut you off in the Third Avenue crosswalk by the Taco Bell. I was never happier to reach my little oasis in the urban jungle.

O'Hale's Bar looked clean, which is to say it was as delightfully filthy and inhospitable as usual. No gods loitered under the flickering neon sign and there was no trace of that SOB in the parka. Still, I am a cautious man by nature when it comes to protecting that most precious commodity under the sun, my ass, and so I made the extra precaution of circling the block and entering O'Hale's through the side door.

The joint was usually pretty dead this time of day. This particular day it was not only dead, it was also undead and — I noted with no small annoyance — reanimated.

The only customers I could see sat a couple of booths away from the door near the busted jukebox. There were three of them, a zombie, a vampire and one of those ambulatory corpses mad scientists are forever piecing together and setting loose on the neighborhood. Every scientist — mad and otherwise — is supposed to get a license from the health department for all projects involving the reanimation of human flesh, but if the crazy ones could be bothered to pull all the right permits they wouldn't be mad. The nuttiest ones never file the right paperwork and, after it all goes horribly wrong and half the city is out chasing their creations with torches, they inevitably dump their monsters in one of the vacant lots over on Burnside along with any used sofas and broken TVs they've got lying around their castles. It's cheaper to heave out a hideously deformed mockery of humanity than pay the five bucks fee to sanitation for a laboratory pickup. Mad scientists are always the cheapest bastards too. It's in their self-mutilated genes.

The dearly departed trio glanced up when I came in. Two of them ogled me like dinner, while the bruiser who'd been assembled in a lab absently picked at the crooked stitches that were holding his giant mauler onto the end of someone else's wrist.

I'd seen the vampire in there a couple of times before, and I flashed my phoniest smile and made a cross with my index fingers. He recoiled, hissing, and flipped me the bird. We understood each other.

The quilt-work golem in the Timberland boots with the four-inch soles wasn't interested in me in the least. The stitched-together monster had a pitcher of beer all to himself and he was crying buckets through somebody else's tear ducts.

"It's not like I *asked* for this," he wailed. "One minute I'm the decomposing corpse of one of my generation's most brilliant academicians, the next I'm waking up on a slab on someone's roof in the middle of lightning storm. I'm not ashamed to say that I pissed my pants. Or *someone's* pants. I have no idea who I am from the waist down. Oh, that a brain like mine could be shoehorned into the body of an oaf like this."

"You not so smart," grunted the zombie. "You sociology professor. Teach at rinky-dink party school. Zombie have you sophomore year. Zombie wind up on dean's list and him either miss most classes or show up drunk whole semester."

The zombie was talking to his sobbing pal at the table, but he only had eyes for my forehead. Frothy foam was already forming at the corners of his gray lips.

"Spool those eyeballs back in their sockets, junior," I warned, tapping a finger to my temple. "This ain't the desert cart."

The vampire tugged on the zombie's ragged sleeve and shook his head. Zombies aren't great for picking up on subtle clues, but this particular ambulatory corpse seemed to get the hint that I was hands-off. He pulled his gaze from my delectable head.

There were only two other people in the joint: the bartender at his usual post, and the waitress who came in some afternoons. She was a solid couple of decades past her sell-by date yet still dressed like the junior prom was next week. The old bird was half-asleep and slouching against the cigarette machine.

The palooka behind the bar had made a point of ignoring my little interaction with his only other customers. When I slid onto my usual stool, Ed Jaublowski, the owner of O'Hale's and the saloon's chief mixologist, pretended he was surprised.

"Oh, hey, Jinx. I didn't see you come in." He was dicing up a quivering brain and dropping the chunks into a blender.

"I'd think, Jaublowski, that a habitual liar like you would at least get marginally better at it after so many years of practice."

The barkeep quit what he was doing and rapidly fixed me up a medicinal bribe. He was moving so fast as he yanked down the bottle and picked up the glass and napkin that for a second I swore he'd sprouted a third arm.

"Whatever, Jinx. Can you just cut them some slack?" He pitched his voice low as he worked. "That rag doll meat-sack must've just gone zombie last night or something. He's got a wallet full of cash he's been flashing around. Usually grave robbers lift whatever they got on them before the voodoo comes around, but they must of missed this guy. He's a *paying* customer. You must've heard of *them*, right? Some people really *do* pay their bartender. So back off, will you?"

It was the most I ever heard Ed talk at once other than the time he was injected with a phonograph needle. Skid row doc mixed up the syringe with a stylus. Jaublowski wouldn't shut up for three days. Worst was the Barbra Streisand numbers he kept belting out. I nearly sank a bullet in my own delicious brain to end that particular torture.

Jaublowski's eyes were pleading as he slid me over a tumbler of turpentine.

"Brains!" the zombie shouted from across the bar, clearly annoyed that the living at O'Hale's got preferential treatment .

"Please, Jinx," Jaublowski begged.

I shook my head and waved my hand in silent acquiescence. Jaublowski quickly snapped the lid on the blender and pureed the hell out of the soggy chunks therein.

"Monkey brains," he explained with a broad wink as he poured the thick mixture into a pitcher. "Zoo always has a pile of 'em left over after the annual barbecue. People'll eat every part these days except the brain, tail and face. Bunch of picky bastards they's raising up nowadays. Not like when we was kids, Jinx. I got thirty pounds of 'em at a steal. Zombie's can't tell the difference, 'specially the freshly turned ones."

"*Brains!*" the zombie bellowed, banging the table.

"Will you, *please*?" hissed his stitched-up monster companion. "You're embarrassing us all." He hissed so emphatically that his lower lip fell off and splashed in his pitcher of beer. "Oh, darn. I am *not* going back up on that roof." He stuck someone's hand inside the beer and fished clumsily around for somebody else's lower lip.

"It is difficult to believe, Ed, that this joint could become even more high class than it has always been," I observed.

"Just please shut up, Jinx, will you?" Jaublowski pleaded.

This time he didn't wait for a reply. The barkeep snapped his fingers and the afternoon waitress roused herself from her slumber. The dame had set the paint gun she used to apply her makeup to two notches above Tammy Faye Baker, and she left the streak of her Bozo profile on the side of the cigarette machine where she'd been snoring.

She earned her day's pay by shuffling the tray with the zombie's pitcher on it over to the booth across the room.

When the waitress returned with the wad of cash, Jaublowski was drooling more than his living dead customer. The waitress went back over to nap against the cigarette machine as Jaublowski hastily rang up the sale and stuffed the dough in the till.

"Ed," I asked nonchalantly as the newly minted King Midas of the barkeep world counted up his ill-gotten gains, "anybody happen to be in here looking for me?"

And just like that Jaublowski's face was suddenly the regular scowling Rosie O'Donnell puss that haunted a thousand city drunks like me in those sweating DT hours between fun and sober. He slammed the register drawer shut.

"What kinda hell you rainin' down on me now, Jinx?" the barkeep demanded.

I shrugged, the very picture of innocence. "Just making conversation."

Jaublowski's reaction alone had already answered my question, and he knew I would be less than forthcoming if he pressed the issue. Over the next silent half hour Jaublowski whipped up a few more pitchers of brains and sent them along with some IV bags of blood to the party at table seven, but his heart — or whatever lump of gnarled muscle in his chest kept him vertical — was no longer in it.

Jaublowski was grinding the smoking blender yet again as I slipped off my favorite stool and shambled off to the toxic cleanup site O'Hale's mislabeled a men's john.

The bathroom was five stalls, three urinals, and no sink, and in a great O'Hale's tradition stretching back decades, the clientele attempted to keep all the porcelain surfaces showroom clean by utilizing the floor for all their hasty evacuation needs.

The O'Hale's men's room was Russian roulette with eight flushable chambers, and I was standing in the middle of the floor and had barely given the cylinder in my head one boozy spin when I heard the door squeak shut behind me.

If there had been a clean surface I would have first looked for a reflection to see who wanted to kill me now, but finding a clean surface in the O'Hale's men's room was as impossible as finding a joke in Jim Carrey's career. Not finding a single reflective surface, I reluctantly staggered around.

My new zombie pal stood just inside the door, a hungry glint in his watery red eyes. He displayed a row of choppers smeared with gray matter and clicked his molars a few times as he eyeballed his half-bagged lunch in the middle of the bathroom floor.

"Brains," he moaned.

"Kid, if mine were anything to write home about, don't you think I'd put them to use locating a gin mill that doesn't use health code violations as wallpaper? Now take it back outside with your pals and you won't live to regret this. Metaphorically speaking, of course. I'm open-minded when it comes to the breathing impaired."

"*Braaaaaaains!*" the zombie persuasively cried.

With zombies it's hard to tell just by looking at them which ones are the fast-movers, and which are the slow shamblers. I got my answer a split-second later when the young zombie darted from the door like a flashing cobra.

He lunged at me, all bared fangs and grabbing arms. Luckily he didn't count on the one-two punch of a surprisingly agile, middle-aged drunk has-been and Jaublowski's crud-covered floors that hadn't seen a mop since O'Hale's was a jitterbugging speakeasy.

I ducked back, hooked my foot around the charging zombie's ankle and let nine decades of sludge-coated linoleum do the rest.

The zombie went down flat and slid hard into the far wall, cracking a dozen tiles and knocking them loose from the mildew-coated walls like busted yellow teeth.

The fast-movers are deadly when cornered, but lucky for me so am I.

I jumped onto the wriggling zombie's back before he was able to flip over and renew his assault. He grabbed blindly for my wrists, like a dirty dog trying to twist out of its master's arms on the way to the bucket of soapy water.

"Brains!" the zombie kid growled, jerking around on his belly, my knee pressed to his spine and pinning him to the floor.

"Just a sec, this is one of those rare occasions that I'm using mine," I informed him.

One scratch from a zombie fingernail and it's a whole quarantine thing if they catch you, then the endless tests and the possibility that you're a zombie now too. Plus the only flesh I felt like hungering for besides Michelle Pfeiffer's was the Banquet spicy chicken wings O'Hale's served alternate Thursday nights. Every way I looked at it was a fresh pain in the ass that I wasn't up for dealing with that day. Only one way out.

I hauled out my piece, planted the barrel at the base

of his neck and blew the bastard to Zombie Heaven, which is actually pretty nice except for all the zombies.

The blowback wasn't so bad; just a little blood and gore on my hands. I didn't have any open wounds that I knew about, but better safe than sorry.

There was a small closet in the men's room near the entrance in which Jaublowski stored cleaning supplies, I assumed as ironic juxtaposition. I found an unopened bottle of ammonia with a price tag from a local supermarket chain that had gone out of business twelve years ago and a bag of Scott paper towels that were so old and yellowed it was like tearing pages from a Gutenberg Bible. I was nearly finished wiping off zombie remains when my virgin ears were assaulted by a string of profanity filthier than the bathroom floor to which my Florsheims were presently welded.

Jaublowski was hollering like he was back dueting with Neil Diamond on "You Don't Bring Me Flowers." I figured he'd gotten a stylus booster from his skid row sawbones but as I reached for the door I suddenly heard the sound of shattering glass.

Fools rush in where angels fear to tread. While I definitely don't have a supply of harp polish and a pair of wings stashed under my mattress, I'm not stupid enough to charge out into the middle of a bar fight without first taking a moment for a little cowardly reconnoitering. I opened the men's room door just a crack.

The idyllic, grimy serenity of O'Hale's had erupted in pandemonium.

The waitress and the stitched-up monster were running screaming out the entrance into daylight. The vampire was gliding for the side door to the apartments that comprised the rest of the building. Jaublowski was behind his bar jumping helplessly from one foot to another as bottle after bottle lining the rear wall exploded in a spray of glass.

Before the bar stood a familiar figure in a white parka.

"Get outta here!" Jaublowski yelled. "What are you, some kinda maniac?"

Parka Man swept the golden trident clutched in his dark hand from left to right, and the next row of bottles popped apart one after the other.

Jaublowski was practically in tears, probably thinking of all the man hours he'd invested in hosing down all that uninsured booze; also how high his water bill — which thanks to his zero tolerance for flushing was usually the basic city sewer charge — was going to shoot up next month throughout the lengthy booze-rewatering process.

"Banyon," Parka Man calmly announced. "Where Banyon?"

I can always count on my pals in a crisis. Jaublowki nearly broke his finger he pointed at the men's room door so hard.

I slammed it shut before the bastard saw me looking out. I stripped off my coat as I ran back across the room. I figured this was going to get hairy fast, and I knew I was right when, as I suspected, the first urinal I ran past exploded in a spray of porcelain. Fat beige chunks scattered like busted bricks across the floor. A corner slab as big as a cinderblock cracked my ankle and sent me spinning side-ways into a stall door.

I hobbled up, then ducked when the second urinal

directly in front of me as well as the bowl behind me erupted simultaneously. A chunk of porcelain the size of my head blasted the closed stall door. I ducked and twisted just in time to see the metal door bend at the waist like a bowing Japanese waiter. The stall vomited out a large chunk of unmoored toilet which slid down the upper half of the buckled door, ripping the metal slab off its hinges. Door and toilet piece crashed to the linoleum.

Water was bursting from busted pipes in three separate locations. The last urinal and the second toilet went up as I ran past. The floor was flooding as I knelt down next to the newly re-dead zombie.

I was already soaked through. A pipe burst on the wall above me and I fought against the tide as I jammed one zombie arm and then the other into my trench coat. Part of a toilet tank had landed nearby, and I busted the handle off with my heel and planted the chrome in the bullet entry wound in the back of the zombie's neck.

I was back up in a flash, slipped, fell, got up in another much more nauseated flash, and ran like hell back across the bathroom.

The last three toilets blasted to pieces on the return trip and I raced the gauntlet of gushing water all the way to the small bathroom closet. I crammed myself inside and yanked the door shut just in time. In the same second I tugged the closet door closed, I heard the bathroom door squeak open.

The door into the bathroom obscured the closet door when it was open, and I was hoping the bow-legged son of a bitch with the trident wouldn't bother with more than a cursory examination. I figured I was right when I heard the door squeak shut a moment later and then heard nothing more over the rush of violent water.

I hid out like a hero for a full minute, and I figured Parka Man had fled the scene when the door squeaked open again and this time I heard Ed Jaublowski's voice.

Jaublowski must've seen the body with the toilet handle compound fracture across the room and come to the same mistaken conclusion as Parka Man.

"Aw, dammit, Jinx," the barkeep moaned.

Jaublowski didn't get all weepy when his old man was snatched by that giant who ground the senior Jaublowski's bones to make his bread, so I knew that his sappy tone had less to do with compassion than it did a lost bar tab with more numbers than a long distance call to Brigadoon. I proved it when I shoved the closet door into the bathroom door and nearly knocked the bastard barkeep down as I stumbled out into the open.

"Jinx!" the bartender snarled, abruptly returned to unpleasant form. "Dammit, Jinx, what the hell?" He looked aghast at the ruins of his bathroom, as if seeing the disaster area for the first time. "You just cost me a goddamn fortune!"

"Look on the bright side, Ed," I offered, slapping my turncoat friend on the shoulder. "For one Judas move on your part, you finally get to break the factory seal on that mop your old lady gave you when you graduated bartending school."

Jaublowski shook off my hand and stumbled out of the bathroom. Water cascaded around his shoes and followed him out into the bar.

I looked across the room at my poor trench coat.

"I am cursed by the simple fact that as a professional fashion statement it looks much better on me," I said, heaving a heavy sigh.

    I couldn't get more sopping wet than I already was. I left Jaublowski spluttering somewhere outside the door like one of his busted pipes and headed back across the crossfire waterfalls to pull my coat off the unanimated zombie bastard lifesaving corpse.

4

Medical Examiner Dr. Harry "Doc" Minto requested the zombie body be loaded up on one of Jaublowski's rickety tables. The water was finally turned off in the O'Hale's men's room, but Doc Minto didn't feel like splashing around in the stagnant pond that still covered the floor. The last time he got down on his knees at a crime scene he snapped two ribs and popped a replacement hip.

The city's chief M.E. was older than Methuselah's grandfather, with skin so pale you could have written a letter on it, pinprick pupils floating behind lenses thick enough to protect a presidential limousine and a dowager's hump so big I figured one day I was going to find an Arab peddling rugs from on top of it.

At least the medical examiner was a smiling face. The only smiles I usually got came from toothpaste ads, my bookie's ugly mug when I emptied the contents of my wallet into his, and that broad on the pancake box.

"You say this happened while you were hiding in a closet?" Doc Minto asked, crinkling his nose. With a green ballpoint pen he tapped the toilet handle that was still jutting from the back of the zombie's neck.

The M.E. was a friend, which was the most rara of

rara avises in my shithole life. The detective the cops sent out, on the other hand, put the ass in bastard.

"Save it, Banyon," Detective Daniel Jenkins snarled. "You can repeat your cock-and-bull story downtown."

Jenkins was relishing holding me there. I was sopping wet, and every dry spot I managed to shuffle onto on the O'Hale's floor quickly dampened from the water that was dripping from the cuffs of my off-the-rack Sears suit pants.

"I was unaware, Detective Jenkins, that being the victim of a crime has become an arrestable offense in this city," I said. "I'll be sure to use my one phone call to inform the *Gazette* of this change in police policy." I flashed him a smile sweet enough to earn me the firing squad from the American Dental Association.

Jenkins stewed for a clenched-jaw moment during which I swore I heard a molar snap, before throwing the previous minute in reverse.

"The Zombie Alex Conner came at you in the bathroom," Jenkins said. He'd found in the zombie's wallet his old ID from when he was a living, breathing sap.

"I already told you all that, Jenkins."

"Indulge me," the flatfoot sneered. "Did you owe him money?"

"The kid was loaded. Ask Jaublowski."

"All the more reason for you to hit him up for a couple of bucks."

"I told you, I never saw him before in my life or in either of his."

"Right," Jenkins deadpanned. He checked his notebook. "So he follows you into the men's room, demands some brains, which—" the flatfoot snorted "—you definitely haven't got to spare, and then the bathroom just starts blowing up, the zombie goes down, and you bravely ride out the storm hiding in a closet."

"You should take up writing professionally, Detective Jenkins. You tell a riveting tale."

Jenkins flipped the notebook shut. "What about the perp in the parka? Jaublowski over there says he was asking for you. He a client?"

"No," I said. When dealing with cops, judges, juries, lie detectors or suspicious wives, it's good to toss in one honest answer once in awhile to keep them guessing.

"Jaublowski says he had some kind of cursed or possessed gardening tool that blew up half his inventory and all the pipes in the bathroom. I suppose you don't know a n y t h i n g   a b o u t   t h a t   e i t h e r ? "
"I know only what you know, Detective Jenkins, at least as pertains to these events. They build libraries to warehouse everything else I know that you don't."

I love the color red I can turn Jenkins' face. It reminds me of Malibu at sunset.

The flatfoot was crushing his notebook in his hand as he marched wordlessly back across the bar to holler some more worthless questions at Jaublowski. The torture I'd inflicted on Jenkins almost made tolerable the squishing of my socks in my dress shoes.

"Back in my day, Crag, a fellow like that would never have made detective," Doc Minto observed in a hoarse whisper. "Terrible what the force has become, even in the little time since you left. All the paperwork, all the fuss. Ladies on the force now. Honest to goodness, Crag. *Ladies*. I ask you, how can they beat a confession out of one of those Elmhurst Ends trolls? You know, the big ones with the mallets and those ears? I'll tell you how. They can't. Don't have the upper body strength. Maybe an imp or a sprite, but never a troll. And I live in that neighborhood. Trolls have taken over. Not safe to walk to that Zimbabwean place on the corner since you left the force a month ago. Best grilled missionary in town, and they're closing next week."

"I quit the cops ten years ago, Doc," I informed him.

He looked up from the zombie corpse that lay sprawled on the table before him and squinted his eyes behind the thick lenses of his enormous glasses. The M.E. said nothing else as he hunched back over the body.

The old buzzard's mind was sometimes a wreck for everything else, but when it came to anatomy he was as sharp as an oni's claws.

Generally, the M.E.'s office would send out the corpse wagon to haul a body back to the morgue. It must've been dead at the office for Doc Minto to come out on a job himself. Not that a zombie constituted much of a job. Most of them had already been processed when they died their living deaths, so if one was revived and then killed in the more permanent, eternal sense a second time later on in zombie form it was usually just a matter of pulling their paperwork and adding a walking dead addendum. Of course, that was different for a licensed P.I. over whom the cops had a collective bug up their ass the size and spitting image of Daniel Jenkins' bastard head..

I'd muffled the shot against the zombie's neck, which I'd only half-expected to work. I hadn't known Parka Man was at that moment giving me cover with Jaublowski and the rest of the crowd out front. In all the confusion nobody knew I'd shot the undead bastard, and until Jenkins showed up I was hoping to slip out without anybody finding out. Unfortunately, Doc Minto was the one man A-team when it came to corpses, and I found out I was right to worry when the old coot stuck a pair of long tweezers down the open neck hole, rooted around for a only a few seconds, and withdrew my spent slug.

"You didn't say anything to Jenkins about firing your piece, Crag," Doc Minto said, clicking his tongue and shaking his head as if talking to a naughty school boy who'd just been caught peeking under the stalls in the girls locker room.

Across the room, the bastard flatfoot looked up when he heard his name.

"You call me, Doctor Minto?" Jenkins snapped.

The medical examiner kept the tweezers holding the slug hidden behind the zombie's body. "No, detective," he called. "I see nothing out of the ordinary here."

Jenkins grunted and resumed interrogating the zombie's vampire buddy under a sun lamp at the end of the bar. The scrawny Nosferatu wannabe's skin was boiling, and he was pleading for a cup of iced blood. The undead lobby was going to have a field day over that one. Last time something like that happened, they protested in front of city hall for weeks. Too bad for them they could only do it at night when nobody was there, then ate all the night janitors and wound up getting the holy water hoses turned on them.

Doc Minto slipped the slug into a baggie and passed it to me.

"Paperwork isn't worth it to me on these cases either, Crag," the M.E. whispered.

He packed up his bag and shuffled for the bar's entrance. "That one can be bagged and processed along to Oscar Meyer," he informed Jenkins on his way out.

I tucked the plastic bag in my suit jacket pocket and was plotting an escape attempt of my own as I casually inched over to where Jaublowski was sitting.

I knew the drinksmith had legs, but I'd seen them so rarely that they had taken on mythical proportions. But there they were, as big as life in a pair of black Dockers. He even had feet at the end of them, but out of respect for his deceased crap palace I didn't mock the shoddy yellow generic Bradlees sneakers that adorned them.

"Hey, Ed, what did that guy in the parka say to you?" I said, softly enough that Jenkins over with his vampire victim didn't hear.

"My insurance ain't gonna cover this, Jinx," Jaublowski moaned. "You got any idea how much booze I gotta peddle to pay for just one shitter?"

"Fortunately, they were more a cautionary hygiene tale than of any practical use in the traditional waste disposal sense. I've even rushed home and cleaned my own bathroom a couple of times in the dead of night after first making the grave miscalculation here that I was loaded enough to toss sanitary sanity to the wind. What about the guy, Ed?"

"Huhn?" Jaublowski said. "Oh. I don't know. I don't remember. He just said he was looking for you, is all."

"Did you get a good look at him? What did he sound like? Anything at all, Ed."

Jaublowski bravely fought past his busted porcelain pain.

"His English wasn't not so good likes you's and me's,"

the barkeep said. "I didn't get a good look at his face. He had on shades, and some of that shit they grease up their nose with at the beach. Dark skin, but like Hawaiian dark, not black. *Hawaiian.* Yeah, now that I think of it, Jinx, he smelled like coconuts."

The bartender couldn't think of anything else. I left him muttering in his chair as I inched back over to the table where Doc Minto had examined the zombie corpse.

The only article of clothing I'd worn into O'Hale's that wasn't soaked through was my hat, which I'd left on the bar when I went to the john, and that was on the table next to the re-dead zombie. My trench coat was slung over the back of one of the chairs, and as I scooped it up I noticed something on the floor under the wobbly table.

The water that washed out from the bathroom had snagged something on its way across the floor. When I was sure Jenkins and none of the other flatfoots were looking, I quickly leaned over and unwrapped the long strand of waterlogged weed that had wrapped around the leg of the table.

"You get a look at the guy from the waist down, Ed?" I whispered to Jaublowski.

The barkeep shook his head. I tucked the length of weed in my pocket alongside the used slug, and when Jenkins chose that precise moment to look up I covered by patting down all my pockets and offering the copper a hopeful shrug.

"You got a spare Jackson, Jenkins?" I asked. "Before all the excitement, I enjoyed several glasses of O'Hale's finest watered-down furniture polish."

"You owe for a hell of a lot more than that," Jaublowski

groaned from the table where he was slouched and staring into the ruins of the O'Hale's Bar men's room.

"Are you out of your mind, Banyon?" Jenkins asked.

I didn't blame him for being appalled that I'd try to bum a twenty. I did, on the other hand, blame the cops for letting an idiot on the force who was easier to play than "Yankee Doodle" on a kazoo.

"Get the hell out of here," the pride of the local constabulary predictably added.

Two birds with one stone. I skipped out on both Jenkins and Jaublowski and hustled through the crummy bar's front door. I rounded the corner near the closed and boarded-up free clinic before either of them could tackle me on the sidewalk.

The sun was burning low in the evening sky, playing peek-a-boo with me as it slid in and out between the saw-toothed skyline of crumbling buildings.

I got a couple of funny looks from people who probably figured I'd pranced through an open fireplug in my suit, but one of the few good things about living in the city is that no one ever stops to see if their fellow man is okay. Good Samaritans who don't want to wind up FBI crime statistics check their halos at the door.

I knew Parka Man wasn't going to be a problem, at least for the time being. The fuzzy SOB thought my corpse was riddled with crapper shrapnel on the floor of O'Hale's. I didn't know for sure what he had against me, but I had a pretty good idea.

I tossed my dead slug in a random trash can on my way back to the office, and took a moment to take another look at the wet weed I'd found on the floor at O'Hale's before sticking it back in my pocket and picking up my pace.

The street outside my office was more or less back to normal. The cops were gone, the booted cars had all been hauled away, and Vincetti's For the Halibut Fish Bazaar was locked up tight. A few seafood fanatics were rattling the front door and peering through the windows into the dark market, and one or two cars slowed down and then took off again, but the message had gone out that the only joint in town still peddling fish was closed pending the old fishmonger's release or execution by firing squad. The latter hinged on whether the judge had ever eaten a slab of Vincetti's three month old fresh salmon steak dipped in Safeway bleach, the specialty of the house.

I had no idea if Mercury was still hanging around, but I didn't see anything god-shaped pacing back and forth beyond the Banjo Invest window.

I snuck into my building by the back and was about to slink up the stairs when behind me the service elevator doors slid open and out came Mannix hauling the wreckage of my office water cooler.

"Oh, hello, Mr. Crag," the elf said. "Have you been down here all afternoon?"

"No, listen. Is that freak with the feathered feet still hanging around upstairs?"

"Mr. Mercury?" Mannix said. "No, he got tired of waiting and left an hour ago."

"Did he leave a message?"

I'd always heard that a message delivered by Mercury was like a summons that had to be delivered in person.

"No. He said he'd come back. He wasn't very happy, Mr. Crag."

"The disposition of deities is of supreme disinterest to me. Let's go."

Mannix nodded enthusiastically. "I just have to put this in the trash."

I grabbed the dollie Mannix had been using to transport my water cooler, opened the nearest basement door — which happened to be the empty office of Robert Johansen, Bastard Landlord, Esq. — and dumped the whole mess inside.

"Fortunately for us, Mannix, this entire dump is trash. C'mon."

The elf reluctantly followed me onto the service elevator. I was sure by the way he leaned out the door and had to yank his head in at the last minute so it didn't get chopped off when the doors closed that he planned to sneak back down and clean up my mess. I, however, thought too highly of him to let him fall into the mundane trap of always doing the right thing. I planned to keep him too busy. I'd carried my trench coat back from O'Hale's, and as we rode up to the third floor I tossed it to Mannix.

"I'm going to need that dry cleaned, pronto, along with everything I've got on. Take it to that Rumanian joint that's always ripping off buttons and bending zippers so they don't work. They're cheap, plus they're the only laundry in town where stuff looks worse coming out than going in. I like that lived-in look."

I took out my apartment keys and tossed them over.

"First run over and get me a change of clothes. Okay, what did you find out about Mrs. Poseidon?"

The elevator doors slid open and I held up a silencing finger. I leaned one eye out of the car, and seeing no naked god messengers with winged feet, I got out. Mannix pumped his little legs as fast as they'd go to keep up.

"I didn't find out a lot, Mr. Crag. There wasn't a lot *to* find out. There was all kinds of stuff online about the wedding. I printed some out and left it on your desk. I got some of her Olympics clippings. There really wasn't much to find from before that."

"Hold that thought."

We were outside my offices. I stood to one side of the door and rapped a knuckle on the glass. There came no responding thunderclaps, floods or bullets, which made it a nice change of pace from the rest of the crap day I'd been having.

The waiting area inside, where Mannix worked and where Doris sometimes stopped in to read vacation brochures, was empty.

Tarps borrowed from the basement covered nearly everything, and I smelled sawdust in the air. When I pushed open my inner office door, I found the floor as well as the front of my desk had been sanded to bare wood.

"I had no choice, Mr. Crag," Mannix rapidly apologized. "The water went everywhere and I couldn't repair the front of your desk without sanding it down."

All my stuff except for my desk and chair was piled up against one wall. The walls had all been scrubbed down and primer spots dotted the plaster. Goddamn efficiency is what you get when you take on an ex-assembly line toy-maker elf.

Anyway, I didn't blame Mannix, I blamed the Poseidons and the water sports-loving hitman they'd turned onto my scent.

As I crossed the newly sanded floor, I fished in my

pocket and removed the strand of weed I'd recovered at O'Hale's.

I dropped my hat to my desk and from my top drawer I pulled out the hunk of plant I'd found across the street where Parka Man had been standing. I nudged aside the sizable folder of information Mannix had collected on Mrs. Poseidon and rolled out both lengths of flora side-by-side on my desk blotter.

I'm no horticulturist. I haven't been a plant aficionado ever since I was a rookie cop and a sergeant from my precinct got swallowed whole by one of those man-eating outer space plants in a seedy florist shop over on skid row. But even my untrained eye could see the pieces of weed I'd rolled out on my desk were identical.

"You know anything about plants?" I asked.

"Only poinsettias," the elf replied. "They're pretty."

"Not terribly relevant at the moment," I told him. "I believe, Mannix, that we are looking at pieces of a grass skirt."

In all three cases I had never gotten a terribly good view of my attacker. The first time I'd seen that the bottom of his coat looked shredded, but hadn't seen why. The second time I was looking down from my office and seeing him at the wrong angle to get a good look below the parka. The third time was in a flash before I shut the bathroom door, and with the lack of decent lighting, which added to the charming demoralizing ambience of O'Hale's, there was no good look then either.

Jaublowski said Hawaiian, and the sunglasses, zinc landing strip on his conk and now a grass skirt hitched up under that parka lent credibility to that speculation. Of course, I had to further take into account that Ed Jaublowski was a moron but, on balance and until further evidence revealed itself, it all still fit.

"So why does a Hawaiian assassin not want me working for Poseidon?" I mused.

"I don't know, Mr. Crag, but if he wants to hurt you he's a very naughty man," Mannix offered helpfully.

I allowed that this was, indeed, naughtier than all hell, which seemed to make the elf happy.

I figured Parka Man, his Ray-Bans, that mangy grass skirt, and the stolen trident he was wielding the shit out of all had something to do with the threatening phone calls and mail the Poseidons claimed they'd been getting. There was still no way in hell I was taking their case, but I resigned myself to the fact that I'd have to talk to them again if only to see what I could find out about my newest pal, the pitchfork-happy maniac. The dame hadn't been forthcoming, but maybe I could get something out of her meathead husband.

"Get that stuff taken care of, Mannix. And if while at my apartment you happen to bump into any gods or assholes waving around magic tridents, be a mensch and don't tell them where I am. My dance card's too full to make room for vivisection tonight."

The elf left, and I heard the outer door to my offices lock on his way out.

I dragged off my damp suit jacket and tie for the second time that day, but when I went to hang them on my coat rack it was gone. I found it out in Doris' office. I left my coat and tie on the displaced rack and went back into my own office.

I scooped up the file Mannix had collected on Miss Ravelli. It was a little thicker than he'd made it sound, but it was still pretty thin by efficient elf standards. I brought it over to the spot where my couch was supposed to be.

"Dammit."

I went to the opposite wall, dumped onto the floor the file cabinets, trash can, window fan, lamps, black and white portable TV, and neat stacks of paperwork Mannix had piled on the couch; I read for nearly twenty full seconds, decided to hell with it, tossed the Miss Ravelli file to the floor with the rest of my office junk and was asleep by the time the second hand reached twelve.

It turned out it was a pretty smart move to get my beauty sleep, since first thing the next morning I was kidnapped by a goddamned god.

5

Near death experiences aren't worse than actual death experiences, but they still take the wind out of a tattered set of a paunchy, middle-aged P.I. sails.

Actually, actual death experiences aren't so bad, provided I'm on the giving and not the receiving end. When I woke up groggy the next morning drooling on my cheap fake leather office couch, it took me a minute to remember that I was not, in fact, deader than de Gaulle after they chased him up the Eiffel Tower and set fire to it.

My elbow had swollen to twice its normal size. My tongue felt like I'd spent the night licking stamps, and my head felt worse than if I'd been sticking them on envelopes stuffed with alimony checks. My clothes were still slightly damp, and there was a disturbing crustiness to the cuffs of my trousers as I rolled over that I hadn't noticed while soaked and which I made the conscious decision to pretend wasn't there.

Mannix had snuck back at some point during the night. A clean set of clothes was laid out on my desk, and he'd scraped up an old blanket somewhere that he'd tossed over me. I tried to kick the blanket off but my joints were being uncooperative, so I did a sort of half-sliding, facedown limbo dance out from underneath it.

Gravity and years of practice helped my feet find the floor, and after a couple of failed attempts I managed to wobble upright.

The elf had somehow managed to remove my shoes while I slept. They were parked on the floor in front of my desk. The residue from Jaublowski's bathroom floor had been chiseled off, and my Florsheims were clean, dry, polished and looking better than they had when I found them on the shelf in the Salvation Army thrift store.

My water cooler was gone thanks to the bastard with the parka, so even half-assed freshening up wasn't possible. I put my clean clothes on over my stale body and hoped that my last real shower before my men's room delousing was up to the challenge of pulling double duty.

I took a look out in Doris' office and found that Mannix had already collected my coat and tie from the rack and replaced them with my trench coat fresh from the worst dry cleaner's in town. It was clean yet exquisitely rumpled. The perfect job. I made the magnanimous decision to give the rotten old war criminal who ran the cleaner's the generous tip of not turning him over to the International Criminal Court at The Hague for being Nicolae Ceausescu.

I finally had the energy to look through the file Mannix had collected on Mrs. Poseidon, and rather than endure the depressing facelift my office was undergoing I brought the file out and read it at Doris' desk, despite the fact that I was a little afraid the poor confused slab of maple might burst into flames from the first actual work that had ever been done on it since it rolled off the showroom floor.

Mannix was right. There wasn't much to the life of Miss Ravelli prior to the Olympics. There were lots of printouts from newspapers about the Russian shark that had eaten the rest of the gals during the 100 meter butterfly. Mannix had found a picture of Olga Toothchenko's dorsal fin with her hammer-and-sickle bathing cap pulled down the tip swimming just two feet from Miss Ravelli, but heading off in the other direction. The caption read "Fish or Foul?" which was a pretty good reminder of why I hate the press.

Those were the last Olympics Miss Ravelli had participated in.

She was young enough to have come back and was apparently a veritable torpedo in the water, and after winning the silver she was expected to return for the Shangri-La games.four years later, so a lot of people were surprised when she opted out. Mannix had found lots of articles speculating that she was afraid to return to the pool after her involvement in the third worst Olympics 100 meter bloodbath in the past twenty years.

I was surprised so much had been written on the subject. A lot of the pieces had been copied from the *Gazette*'s online archives. I read the sports page of the local rag as often as I'm able to steal a copy, yet I'd never seen a single one of these pieces on Miss Ravelli when they'd originally run. I assumed they must have all been on some fruity human interest page or mixed in with the comics, since swimming is basically taking a really fast bath with your underwear on and doesn't count as an actual real sport.

Every self-proclaimed expert who said she was afraid to swim again was as wrong as know-it-all assholes usually are. She participated in all kinds of charity water events after the Olympics, and even met her future husband just like she told me, halfway across the English Channel. The waterlogged saps were engaged before they reached Calais.

If that was what being afraid to go into water was like, I'm terrified the exact same way of liquor stores. Where's my goddamn Jerry Lewis Telethon?

Prior to the Olympics, her life story got thinner than Lara Flynn Boyle's thorax.

She was born in Kansas. Parents dead. No siblings. Mannix had even gone through the video promo spots NBC posted online during the Olympics, and the elf made a couple of notes. No relatives ever cheered her on at any events, she never even mentioned so much as a single distant cousin back home. The blank slate life story of Miss Ravelli sounded like somebody trying to erase her past, and had even roused suspicion in Mannix. He had written "naughty?" in the margin, but he thought that of pretty much everyone he ever met except (for some horribly inaccurate reason) me.

There was stuff on the wedding, but I got bored with that fast. Nothing but puff pieces about the happy couple, some trouble she had getting a dress to fit her butt and legs properly, an allergy she had to the flowers that almost postponed the wedding, the groom's family friction that would keep his side of the Sunken Cathedral empty.

Taking each article individually, there was nothing there. Cumulatively, I got a pretty clear picture of a dame with something to hide.

I looked in Doris' main desk drawer for a pencil to write Mannix a note, but all I found was lip gloss and back issues of *Entertainment Weekly*. One side drawer held nothing but worn-out emery boards and empty nail polish jars.

"I would fire you, Doris, but I'm not quite sure what you do here technically qualifies as work," I informed the strawberry blonde wig in her bottom drawer.

(Plus since I rarely paid her we were in a gray area as far as official employment as it is generally understood by the United States government.)

I was heading back into my office when I heard a familiar crack of thunder and saw the flash of light on the other side of the closed and locked door to my suite. A cloud of dust from the gale force wind that heralded Mercury's arrival burst beneath the door.

The doorknob started rattling like a bastard.

"Banyon! You in there?"

There was a rap on the door and all I caught was the brief silhouette of a god in muscle-bound human form through the translucent glass as I grabbed up my trench coat and ran for my inner office. I snatched my hat from my desk and ten seconds later I found myself bounding down the rusted fire escape for the second time in two days.

I made it only one floor down. I was passing the windows of Shyster, Pilfer & Fraud, the downstairs law firm whose senior partners had hilariously accurate yet entirely coincidental names, when there was another brilliant flash of light, this time through the window immediately beyond the aching bruise of my injured elbow. It was accompanied by another ostentatious thunderclap, and I briefly saw the terrified fat face of Schmecky Shyster, ambulance chaser-at-law, who had been in the process of testing out a Swindler 2000 neck brace around his own bullfrog throat. Paperwork blew like an indoor snow squall around the office, and through the maelstrom I saw a very large hand connected to an arm with a glandular problem smashing through the glass behind the lawyer's desk.

The hand grabbed my coat collar, shattered glass flew everywhere, and for a split second I considered slipping out of my trench coat and continuing on my merry, cowardly way. But after fifteen years I'd only just finally started breaking it in and I hated the thought of wasting weekends picking through flasher estate sales for a replacement.

And in that tiny second of hesitation, the rest of the window's glass came crashing out along with most of the frame, and I was joined on the fire escape by a nearly naked Greek god with feathers on his shoes and a letter in his hand.

"You're Banyon, " Mercury grunted.

"I plead the fifth on the grounds that whatever I say could get me murdered and tossed into traffic. You heard me, Schmecky," I called to the lawyer through the remains of his office window. "You want the case? I can't promise cash, but candy canes can possibly be arranged. I have a source."

Shyster finally found the voice that had sunk a thousand court cases, screamed like a banshee as he tossed the neck brace in the air, and ran like hell from his office, his ass, gut and chins jiggling like an all-girl marching band.

"No doubt conferring with senior partners Pilfer and Fraud on the major case he just landed for the firm. I wouldn't want to be in your shoes, legally speaking. Frankly, not just legally speaking. Those wings aren't a look that would work for me. You, however, not only manage to sell it, you look exceedingly manly in the process."

"Shut up, Banyon," Mercury said. "Read this."

Nothing delivered to me by the messenger of the gods could possibly be good news. Hell, for two years a decade ago I tossed all of my regular USPS mail straight in the incinerator under the sensible assumption that any checks were purely theoretical since my clients mostly stiffed me, and any checks that might be there would be more than offset by bills. It was a kind of perfect postal equilibrium. But when Mercury stuffed the letter in my hand, folded his arms over his gym rat chest and stood there watching me like the last candy bar in the vending machine, I had no real choice.

I popped the wax seal on the letter and shook it open.

It was set up exactly like formal business correspondence no longer is. The previous day's date was at the top and the inside address identified me as Mr. Crag Banyon, President of Banyon Investigations, Incorporated.

"It's possible this is meant for a Crag Banyon from another dimension," I informed Mercury, "since I've never once referred to myself as 'president.' I'm more the 'if nominated, I will not accept; if elected, I will not serve' type. The good news is that I've had some cross-dimensional experience, so I suggest you engage my services to search for myself. I can have my office elf start drafting up the paperwork and we can get something out to you in the mail in fifty or sixty years."

He was still clutching the collar of my trench coat and there was no strain on his face as he raised his arm. My feet left the fire escape and my toes dangled.

"Read," insisted the stubbornly single-minded messenger of the gods.

I read the entirety of the note aloud. "'I want to talk to you.'"

I flipped it over. There was nothing on the back except the remains of the wax seal. The note had the "Very Truly Yours" complimentary closer along with the typed name "Zeus" below the god's signature, which would probably fetch a bundle on eBay.

"Not one for lengthy communication, is he?" I said. "I admire that in a deity. Have you seen this Bible they've got now? Showed up after your time. Thing weighs a ton and could be summed up in one phrase: 'knock it off.' Okay, have Zeus' people call my elf and we'll set something up. How does a decade from next Tuesday sound?"

I could see from the scowl that he wasn't buying. If he'd given me the chance, I could've run to the paper supply store to pick up a pocket calendar so we could sit down and hash out a firm date for a meeting that I most definitely planned to skip out on. Instead he dropped my soles back to the fire escape and wound his hand tighter into the collar of my trench coat.

There was a flash of light, a roar of thunder that felt like it was blasting straight through one ear and out the other, and the fire escape below my feet and the grimy sandstone wall with the blown-out window vanished into nothingness.

6

Being transported through a vortex of thunder and light against your will is a little like being stuffed alongside a million-watt light bulb and a sack full of cats into a dryer set to spin at a hundred miles an hour. The whole trip took a fraction of a second and when we exited the far end and landed back on solid ground I felt like I'd been drawn through a thousand mile-long Silly Straw. Mercury, on the other hand, looked none the worse for wear and very annoyed.

"This would've gone easier if you hadn't dodged me yesterday, Banyon," the messenger god informed me.

I doubted any consequence of Mercury's surprise initial visit would be easy on me, which was why I'd done my unsuccessful best to dodge him, and at that moment I had fresh reason to doubt the accuracy of his declaration.

We had been teleported to Greece. I could tell by all the crumbling columns that weren't holding up the crumbling roofs of the crumbling buildings. Plus the whole dump reeked of feta cheese and olive oil and there was a guy across the road putting lipstick on a goat.

The ancient Greeks were so proud of all their sophisticated architecture, philosophy, literature, sodomy and math that when they were through they all took one giant pederastic step back to admire a job well done. In the couple thousand years they'd been loitering around waiting for the paint to dry on the Parthenon, their whole civilization had collapsed into postcard-perfect picturesque ruins.

I had a grammar school teacher who was obsessed with Greek history. Mrs. Crapadopoulis told us a million times how that phrase about faith moving mountains came from the ancient Greek gods. See, at first the gods were like young Mel Gibson: huge for a time and everyone loved them. But eventually they were like old Mel Gibson: jerk-offs. Once bacchanal attendance started dropping off, the faith that the gods still had in themselves moved Mount Olympus smack-dab into the heart of Athens. The deities figured the Greeks couldn't forget about them if they had to steer their chariots around them every morning on the way to work at the statue factory.

Olympus had been moved two thousand years ago, and a lot had changed since then. These days every business in Greece was boarded up, the entire population of the country was on a cradle-to-grave vacation, and the Greeks had run out of people to stick with the ouzo and KY bill. Apparently now that their social Ponzi scheme was collapsing around their hairy ears they'd finally turned back to their old gods.

Mercury and I had materialized on the slopes around Mount Olympus and right in the middle of the biggest domestic protest since PETA tried unsuccessfully to ban the fundamental human right a man had to marry the sheep of his dreams.

There were thousands of sweaty Greeks screaming bloody murder, every one of them waving a placard in my face. I might not understand Greek, but I am well-versed in the international language of lazy slack-ass.

The protestors were chanting protest songs and throwing rocks up at the marble buildings on the mountain. The buildings started about a mile up, and there's a reason why there are no Greek pitchers in the big leagues.

Chariots rode through the multitude, one union bureaucrat holding the reins while another in the back passed out baklava and government checks. Free money didn't satisfy Yannis Q. Publicas. Everyone presented with a check just got angrier and, after they ate the complimentary pastry, wound up looking around for more rocks to heave.

Mercury and I had to fight our way through the edge of the crowd. In twenty feet I had to deck five Greeks whose hands somehow managed to make it into my pockets.

"They don't seem all that delighted to see you," I said to Mercury, who had just put his fist through the head of a twenty year old protestor who'd tried to steal the wings from the messenger god's sissy shoes.

"We are gods," Mercury sniffed, as if divinity paid the gas bill.

I was guessing that holier-than-thou schtick would last only as long as the thunderbolts held out. I saw charred areas around the base of the mountain as we broke from the edge of the crowd. Judging by the gore, bones, and tacky gold chains scattered around each black patch, I figured everyone who strayed too far out of line was blasted to fried zucchini by a bolt launched down from on high.

There was a marble platform to service a golden tram near the base of the mountain, and Mercury gave a little hostile nod that I should get on the car.

It was air conditioned inside. I'm pretty sure it was Yanni playing over the speakers. Under ordinary circumstances I would have shot them out, but the replacement cost for solid gold Bo Bengtssons is out of my humble P.I. price range. Also, I suddenly realized that I'd never reloaded after I'd taken out that zombie at O'Hale's, and I figured now wasn't the best time to play music critic with the last five rounds to my name.

The tram moved fast and silent, and we quickly left the screaming crowd far below us. It still didn't move fast enough for flyboy Mercury. He was pacing around the car like a caged centaur on St. Gelding's Eve.

"I gather there's some rule about mortals not being able to materialize up top," I said as we passed a grove where some gardeners were fighting over a golden apple.

"I must deliver you, for that is my immortal purpose," Mercury said. "But, yes, your presence is forcing this indignity on me, Banyon."

"Yeah, I'm an indignity magnet. Hey, on a completely unrelated note, not many straight gods could pull off this whole ballet slippers and dish towel look." I gave him a very big wink and a confident thumbs-up. I really am the king of the assholes.

Mercury apparently didn't take compliments too great, but luckily looks don't smite so I wasn't a pile of smoking ash when the doors opened at the summit.

Mount Olympus was like a tackier Atlantic City, with

temples instead of casinos and about an equal number of whores per square foot.

The dames that wandered the marble streets all had the same vacant look I'd seen on countless faces of young girls who'd come to the big city banking on making a name for themselves only to find fame fickle and fortune something they serve in a cookie at P.F. Chang's along with a side order of heartache. These wrecks probably showed up at the bus depot in Athens with heads full of big city dreams, only to wind up in some temple in the hills snorting souvlaki off the chrome coffee table of some skeevy lowlife forest god. Next thing you know they've got a deal with Eros Pictures for three movies a week, but they swear it's only for the drachmas to make the rent until their winged horse finally swoops in. Before they know it, it's twenty years later and they're dried up like the springs of the Argolid and stumbling around the streets of Mount Olympus, half of them towing snot-nosed demi-gods in their wakes and begging for just a cupful of ambrosia for child support.

The sidewalks through which the tramps shuffled didn't give much room for anyone to move. The streets were clogged with piles of gilded trunks, casks of wine, and gold and silk furniture up the wazoo. Leaning against a nearby building was a line of olive trees that had been ripped from the ground, their root balls wrapped in burlap. Tons of luggage was already loaded in the backs of dozens of giant rented U-Haul chariots, but the horses weren't yet yoked up. Obviously there was a major move coming for Olympus, and by the looks of the junk piled out in the streets it was going to be soon.

Whatever was going on to force the move, whether

it was by choice or because of the mob down below, the gods were definitely losing their security deposit.

The majestic temples that adorned the mountain had been magically created way back when the Olympus gods kicked the Titans to the curb. Magic is fun for party tricks, but it doesn't take the place of a full-time janitorial staff. No one had been out with a ladder and a bucket of soapy water in centuries, and so the grubby temples had aged about as well as the mortal streetwalkers who staggered around among them.

Flashing neon on the side of the biggest building announced it was the Temple of Zeus in about twenty languages. But the sign buzzed like a son-of-a-bitch, the Z was crooked and hanging off, and the M was burned out completely. A family of squawking stymphalians nested in the valley of the dead M, and they were pecking the hell out of the marble with their bronze beaks and crapping a shit storm down the front of the building.

The marble of the temple looked dingy, the joints wept grime and there were lesser gods that mankind's lost faith had rendered obsolete either pushing shopping carts filled with tin cans and nectar or sleeping like bums on the steps. The whole joint could have used a can of Spic and Span, some elbow grease and the nearest convenient river redirected through it.

As Mercury led me up the steps, a strung-out muse offered to inspire me for spare change. The messenger god shoved her aside.

"Oh, yeah, like you is so special there, Mercury!" she screamed at our backs. "You ain't nuthin', see! I wouldn't inspire you to write an ode to a nymph cavorting in a forest spring if you was the last god in the whole goddamn pantheon, ya lousy bum!"

She was hollering something about dewdrops clinging to newly-formed leaves that he could shove up his ass as Mercury kicked the golden front doors open and pushed me inside the temple.

The place was one huge, drafty hall with a giant pedestal on which was a golden throne. There, lounging casually high above the floor, was the god himself.

He looked younger than his statues, and at some point he'd lost the beard. By the looks of the rest of him, I was guessing about 1975.

Zeus' orange velour shirt had billowing sleeves and was unbuttoned to the navel. The open V of the front of his shirt revealed a carpet of simian fur and a dozen tacky gold chains. Similar bling dangled from thick but slightly fey wrists. His skintight, powder blue slacks looked like they'd been applied with an aerosol can, except for the flaring bellbottom cuffs which were decorated with rings of garish rhinestone detailing.

If I'd tried standing up in white platform shoes with soles that thick, I'd've wound up with a nosebleed and plugged ears. Then I would have tossed my sorry, cross-dressing Foxy Brown ass off the side of the mountain.

"Mr. Banyon!" Zeus called down merrily, flashing a set of pearly white teeth in a dark, suntanned face. "Can I offer you something? Honey? Laurel? Jelly filled?"

He gestured to the ceiling where a continuous stream of doves flew through narrow openings, lugging cups of takeout coffee and bags of Krispy Kremes.

The birds dropped the coffee and doughnuts into the hands of other gods who were hanging around the main floor of the temple and looking like they were trying to

reenact a slightly less decadent tableau vivant of Andy
Warhol's The Factory. All the bastard members of the
lounging god group were trying way too hard to look
indifferent, like they'd just happened to wander in off the
luggage-clogged street.

High above us all, Zeus clapped his big hands and
tried to wave a pigeon to drop a honey glazed my way.

"I'm good," I said. "Other than the fact that you had
your goon here kidnap me and in the process trash the
offices of a ferocious, fat ambulance chaser. I'm deeply
looking forward to the lawsuit for emotional distress and
destruction of property Schmecky Shyster, attorney-at-
scam, has no doubt already waddled out and filed against
me."

Zeus hopped lightly to his feet and began descending
to my level. The guy was at least as big as Poseidon, but
looked more world weary than his brother.

A harem of played-out mortal Greek skanks lounged
on the steps leading up the front of the pedestal, and they
earned their keep at that moment oohing and ahing and
being generally awestruck at the extreme studliness of
the disco-era lounge lizard who passed through their
coked-out midst.

"Nomos, the spirit of the law, will be on your side,"
Zeus assured me, towering over me at nearly seven feet
and nodding wisely. "Just let the girl know when your
court date is and I'll send him along. But not Fridays. He
has AA."

Zeus wrapped an arm around my shoulder.

"I ordinarily don't meet with mortals like this," the
big chief god assured me.

"And I'd ordinarily punch a guy in the throat for

fondling my shoulder blades. It's apparently a day of firsts."

Zeus grinned an oily, phony grin that really should have merited him a sock to the kisser, but I didn't feel like living out the remainder of eternity rolling a boulder up and down my apartment stairs.

Up close his eyes were bloodshot. I had to hand it to him. Thousands of years of miles on the odometer, yet he still loved the nightlife and had to boogie. Disco bastard.

"I got a message my brother Poseidon hired you, Mr. Banyon."

"If it came from Western Union here, he got his wires crossed," I said, nodding to Mercury. "We talked, I didn't take the job. End of story."

Zeus shot a glare at Mercury, and for an instant fire flashed in the bleary eyes. The messenger god shrugged and gave a "beats me" frown.

"Well, that's good," the god of the skies said to me, that creepy affable smile returning. "Mortals who get involved in Olympus business tend to get the shit end of the stick, as it were. It's unfortunate, granted, but we've got our ways and you have yours."

Throughout it all he kept his arm clamped tight around my shoulder, but his grip suddenly tightened and for a second he got distracted by something only a god could see.

Zeus abruptly released me and brought one hand out before him, palm flat and parallel to the floor. He very slowly turned the hand over, closing up his fingers as he flipped it around. As his hand turned, a tiny ball of flame appeared at the center of his palm and by the time his hand had fully turned around the fire had flashed to the size of a softball. The ball of flame sprouted two points that stretched from opposite poles, elongating the orange fire in both directions until it had transformed into a jagged yellow javelin of pure electricity.

Zeus hauled back and hurled the spear. The thunderbolt soared to the ceiling, zapped a dove along the way, and flew out one of the small openings at the roofline. I heard it crackling off into the distance, and when the boom came seconds later it returned as a far distant rumble that barely shook the marble beneath my feet. The fully cooked squab landed smoking halfway across the room.

"Protestors," the head god apologized. "They have no appreciation for private property. No boundaries, Mr. Banyon. Men and gods *must* respect boundaries or the whole world…well, the world becomes like it is, I'm afraid. I'm glad *you* respect boundaries, Mr. Banyon. This business with my brother. What did he say it's about?"

"While your brother and his wife aren't clients, they did consult with me. I make it a point not to discuss that stuff either, unless I mistakenly do so while very drunk or if somebody's beating me up. And while I pride myself on my integrity, I'm open to bribes provided I can reconcile them with my conscience and/or checking account."

"We won't go there," Zeus assured me. The hand was back on my shoulder again, giving me another creepy warm squeeze, but this time he was leading me back to the front door. "I respect you too much, Mr. Banyon."

"You can respect me with your pants on, right?" I asked. He ignored me.

"I'm sorry to have wasted your time, Mr. Banyon.

You may ride the tram down to the platform, at which point you'll be transported back home. We have a gift shop if you want to do a little shopping first. Duty free, since you'll be teleported back to the same location where you were picked up." He offered a broad wink of one very tan eyelid. "I won't tell if you don't. I'm afraid sightseeing is limited to the marked areas, but as long as you've come all this way you may take in the glory that is ancient Olympus, provided you leave at closing time. There'll be an announcement. Tips are welcome."

We were through the doors and standing between a pair of columns that framed the square below the big cheese Greek god's temple. From that vantage point, there was no missing the mounds of luggage and tchotchkes dumped out in the street.

"By the looks of it, I'm not the only one leaving," I said.

Zeus' tan face grew stern. "Yes. The luggage. Well, it's no secret. The mob down below…excuse me." Another ball of fire transformed to another hurled thunderbolt, followed by another distant boom. "Little pricks will never learn. What was I saying? Oh, yes. The people of Greece have bled each other and the rest of the EU dry, and now they've turned to what they think, mistakenly I might add, is the last source of wealth in the country they can confiscate for their goddamn endless summer. Except as far as per capita income on Olympus goes, we're in the red worse than them. I can tell you exactly how many pigs they've slaughtered to me as offertories in the past century." He held up one hand, index finger and thumb forming a circle. "A big, fat golden goose egg, Mr. Banyon. Those idiots down there think we're the last money tree

they can shake. I've done about a hundred TV and newspaper interviews from Athens to Cyprus explaining that
we Olympian gods stopped living on our interest centuries
ago and have been slowly eating away at our principal.
We haven't earned squat up here since they stopped caring
about us. But reasoning with a mob is impossible. They
don't believe it. We're gods, we must be loaded. I only
wish I had Warren Buffett money."

"Tough break. I get the same thing all the time. People
see my fabulous life of excess and intrigue and assume
I'm the Sultan of goddamn Brunei. I take it by all the
packing that you're planning on leaving the mountain
behind when you go."

"Yes, yes," Zeus said, glancing around at the ancient,
faded glory over which he presided. "When enough people
had enough faith in us, we had sufficient faith in ourselves
to move Olympus here to Athens. But once the people
lost their faith…well, let's just say that a lot of the gods
around here have adopted a real Hypnos attitude."

I could see he thought he was being clever, but I didn't
know what the hell he was talking about. Zeus realized
he was talking to yet another mortal who was only vaguely
familiar with the headliners but had no idea who was in
the warmup act.

"Right," the god said, clearing his throat. "Anyway.
So we're moving the conventional way. Flying horses,
magic chariots. Clearing as much out as we can and
leaving what's left for the lazy vultures down below to
pick through after we're gone. I only hope they choke on
a cornice."

He sent out a couple of wild thunderbolts that had
nothing to do with crowd control. When the twin thumps

came, I knew that there were a couple of newly empty, smoking beach chairs somewhere in the 365-days-a-year vacation crowd far below.

"Yeah, it's tough all over, buddy," I said, inching out of his shadow and backing down the stairs. "I'd put in a good word for you at my place, but the super's such a no-pets fanatic that he'd never make an exception even for randy deities who transform into livestock to impress the chicks. Bastard'd chase you out the front door with a broom the first time you forget to change back and he found you in ram form sorting through your mail in the downstairs hall. Too bad, but that's life. See you in the funny papers."

"Oh, we already have somewhere in mind," Zeus said.

The mysterious tone people use whenever they think they know something you don't gets me every time. Of the top three things that'll get me killed, my goddamn curiosity is number two on the list. (Number three is being seltzered to death by a mob of Albanian circus clowns, at least according to the buggy police fortune teller who did all our readings back when I was on the force. Number one is spontaneous liver detonation.)

I very casually stopped halfway down the stairs.

"Relocating the whole outfit to someplace more hospitable to free market principals than Greece, are you?" I said. "I'm sure you'll flourish in North Korea."

"We were actually looking into a couple of places. This new 'holy land' of yours sounded promising. I mean, we're gods and all, so that seemed ideal. But, hell, we looked into it and that's worse than Greece. For a little while Trump was going to put us up at some new spot in the desert. Like a theme place, built specifically around us. But he wanted three shows a night out of me. That's bulfinch, man. I'm not going back on the boards at my age. So that fell through too. But we found a spot."

"Poseidon—"

Zeus had been staring out across his crumbling domain as he spoke, and most of what he said was to himself. When I mentioned his brother's name, he snapped out of the trance he'd been in and glanced down at the scrawny little mortal with the big mouth in the trench coat standing on his front stoop.

"—he said he's missed every meeting you guys have had in the past hundred years," I continued. "Ever since that ankle monitor went on. Does he know about the big move the rest of you are taking?"

Zeus offered a tight, tan smile. "I'm glad for *your* sake that you're not taking his case, Mr. Banyon. I'll be sure to have you put in the Rolodex just in case I ever need someone to rattle around in garbage cans looking for hotel receipts. Goodbye."

The big kahuna of all the Greek gods turned on one giant platform heel and marched back inside his temple, slamming his door with a clap of solid gold thunder.

I'm not the Disneyland type, and not just because they found out recently that the guys in the Mickey and Minnie costumes were actual giant talking plague rats from Sumatra. (The whole park had to be sealed off and firebombed. Instead of rebuilding, they reopened a week later and renamed the entire smoldering dump Conceptual Art Land. I heard they're cleaning up with the pretentious college artist crowd who see everything from their depressing, pampered childhoods to their bleak love lives, to the post-American World of Tomorrow Today in the smoking ruins. Disney bastards.)

I don't go in for theme parks, and that goes double for ones run by grabby Greek god perverts whose outfits come from the *Saturday Night Fever* wardrobe trailer.

I couldn't get off Mount Olympus fast enough. I had made it through the thickest cluster of temples and had the tram platform back in sight when I noticed a small marble building with the words Gift Shoppe chiseled above the door.

In the window was a golden fleece wrapped around a Venus mannequin with no arms, a Parthenon snow globe, plus a bunch of cheap plastic statues of various gods. I would've hustled right past if a hand-painted sign on the door hadn't read "Hephaestus, Smith to the Gods, Proprietor. Est. 800 B.C. No sandals, no tunic, no service."

I was still one bullet short, and who knew how far up the mountain the crowd of angry, lazy, horny Greeks might have inched? I didn't feel like meeting that mob without a full chamber, so I ducked in the weapons god's shop.

The blacksmith was sitting naked on a marble slab with a blanket strategically draped over his junk. Beside him was a Formica counter with a cash register, a can stuffed with mutton-flavored Slim Jims, a stack of *Daily Diddler* newspapers and an empty "take a drachma, leave a drachma" tray.

"What do you want?" the naked guy with the blanket on his lap asked.

"First and foremost, I emphatically want you not to stand up. I want to make that abundantly clear. Second, do you have any of these?"

I popped open my piece and shook out a single slug, which I held up for the god in the blanket to examine. The view apparently wasn't good enough from where he was sitting, and the next thing I knew he was up, his blanket was down, and I was doing a lot more sightseeing than I'd bargained for when I woke up on my couch that morning.

"Eh. Primitive. Mortal. Give me a challenge why don't you?" He grabbed the slug out of my hand and wandered through a curtain behind the counter.

I heard some pounding of metal on metal, a little grinding, and he came back out two minutes later with a pair of matching slugs which he dumped on the counter. Lucky for me, the counter blocked the view south of the equator.

He rang up the order on the register, which turned out to be one of those magical Hobart deals that automatically converts to the buyer's national currency.

"Oh. American," he said with a frown, like the dollar was the last currency he felt like dealing with. "Laugh at Greece all you want, you people are next." He took my cash and kept right on making small talk as he searched blindly around the slots with his fingers for change. "America, huh? Ever been to Mount St. Helens?"

"I was married to it for six years," I offered helpfully.

"I'm just glad we're not moving there. My idea. Well, it would be, wouldn't it? Vulcan, god of volcanoes. Vulcan, that's me. Forget the sign out front. I prefer what the Romans called me. Some of us do. Anyway, I suggested St. Helens 'cause I've gotta root for the home team and all, doncha know. Yep. Still glad it was shot down though."

"Yeah, Zeus told me all about the big move," I lied. "You don't have a lot of time to pack this place up by…" I snapped my fingers, like the day had slipped my mind.

"Tuesday morning, rain or shine," Vulcan said. "Maybe sooner if we're lucky, and it looks like we will be, but definitely by then. Not that I'll be taking any of this. Not likely to have many customers where we're going."

"Right," I said. "Not to mention how would you keep a forge burning at the bottom of the sea?"

Most wild stabs in the dark harpoon nothing but empty air. Then there's those hen's teeth-rare, one in a million, home run times where you manage to stab straight through Zombie Hitler, Zombie Stalin and Rosie O'Donnell while simultaneously tripping over a full case of Glenfiddich 30. (Still my best Christmas ever.)

"Oh, I'll have the forge up and running no matter what," Vulcan assured me. "Yep, that won't be a problem. I'm the only one licensed to make weapons for the gods of Olympus. *Formerly* of Olympus next week, I suppose. End of an era. Anyway, it's not just metalwork. Zeus doesn't pull those thunderbolts out of his ass, no matter what it looks like with that flashy act of his. It's just getting down there. Mortals can hike up the mountain to here, but they can't get down there easy. No sense opening up a gift shop at the bottom of the sea if your only customers are shipwrecked ghosts and kraken."

"Yeah, that's a tough break, pal," I agreed. "If it were up to me I'd recommend your courteous, naked service to all my friends. Unfortunately, I don't have any."

I wasn't the only one. I don't know how long lonely old Vulcan had been sitting naked and alone in his gift shop, I just knew that once you pried the conversational lid off this guy he was like a bucket of tipped-over paint slopping all over the floor

"My talents have been going to waste for years anyway," Vulcan lamented. "I see you've got your eye on this." (I had been doing my best not to have my eye on anything, so he actually pointed out something I hadn't seen.) "Amazing little device to a mortal like you, I'm sure. I wager you've never come across one of these before."

The item he was so interested in getting me interested in sat on the end of the counter on the other side of the register. It looked like an ordinary fishbowl, with the requisite two goldfish swishing around inside like the lazy gold bastards they are. He insisted that I lean in over the thing and give it a bird's eye view.

When I looked down over it, I saw that there was a hollow center, like looking straight down through one of Zeus' Krispy Kremes. I figured the bowl had a glass core to hold the water from the middle, but Vulcan stuck his arm straight down the center and withdrew a metal circle from the bottom. When he pulled his wet arm out, the hollow center was gone. The water had washed in from the sides and flooded the middle. A fish swam directly through the area where a moment before there had been nothing but air.

"Nifty, eh?" Vulcan said, holding out for inspection the item he'd extracted from the bottom of the bowl.

It was as thin as one of those pieces of cardboard they stick in new dress shirts to keep them neat in the plastic wrapping, assuming they still shove cardboard inside new dress shirts. I haven't bought a new shirt since they opened a consignment shop at the state prison. Two dress shirts for the price of one if the owner got the chair. Great deal and fewer burn holes than a normal trip to my usual crummy laundry.

The circular hunk of metal looked like an oversized washer made of bronze, and when Vulcan returned it to the bowl I watched the water recede and the hollow tube reform up the middle like the Red Sea magically parting. Vulcan put his arm down into the bone dry center of the fishbowl and stuck his index finger into the water from the middle of the H2O bundt pan. He jiggled the tip, frightening a goldfish.

"That's artistry, that is," Vulcan assured me. "It pushes water aside and creates a boundary between it and the oxygen up the middle. The fish won't come through. Won't even try. To them it's a scary wall they stay away from. I understand you mortals do something similar with dogs and invisible fences. Should have filed a patent, but who knew you'd get so clever? In my day you couldn't even come up with fire on your own."

"Don't look at me, I never touch the stuff," I assured him. "Although the distillation process I rely on for my daily sustenance would be negatively impacted if you decided to demand it back from Mr. Jim Beam. Tell you what. Let humanity keep fire, and you can sell me one of those little gizmos you got there."

Another sale thrilled the naked forger god, and as a bonus probably distracted him from my earlier line of brilliantly subtle inquiry.

I'd learned everything from Vulcan that I could without

risking him catching on and running off to rat me out to the captain of the Thessalonica thunderbolt hurtling team. But there were still two vitally important questions I had to ask him.

"Those bottles on the shelf behind you. How much of a going-out-of-business discount will you give me and, of equally essential magnitude, can you reach them without moving your ass and other assorted parts away from that counter?"

7

Mannix apparently heard the commotion coming from outside and came to the fire escape window to see what all the hollering was about. He was happy to see me, as always, and eagerly took the bags of clanking bottles that I passed in to him.

"That was very bad language I heard someone yelling," the elf said.

"Just fatso Shyster downstairs in twelve," I said as I climbed inside the lovely home I'd kindly given to my adopted bottles of marked-down, tax-free booze. "He says me reverse-dematerializing outside his broken window just now nearly gave him a heart attack, which he is very kindly adding to the case that's going to bankrupt me. Hey, swell job on the desk."

In my absence, Mannix had finished repairing the holes the exploding water cooler had Swiss-cheesed into the front of my desk. The kid had stained, lightly buffed, then battered the hell out of the woodwork until it was as lousy-looking as ever.

"I was worried when I came in this morning and found that folder on Miss Doris' desk," the elf said, nodding with deep concern to the outer office.

"I can understand why you'd panic at evidence of work possibly being attempted anywhere in the vicinity of where Doris and her portable nail salon roost. It's human nature to feel apprehension when faced with the extraordinary." I dropped in my chair. "Mercury came back," I explained. "He abducted me to Greece where the king of all gods on Earth made a few not-so-veiled threats. Then I did a little shopping."

"Oh," Mannix said, nodding somberly for as many seconds as he could bear before adding brightly, "Did you bring me anything?"

I reached into one of the bags and tossed him a box. "Chocolate covered roasted almonds, which sound about as nauseating as you like. Bon cavities."

The elf clutched the box happily to his heart. "Did you get anything for Miss Doris?"

"Yeah, a job to come back to that she stinks at and won't do. About that file on her desk. The stuff you collected on Poseidon's wife is pretty thin pre-Olympics. I'm going to need you to do a naughty or nice check on her with your pals at the Pole."

Mannix clenched his jaw, clicking his pointed teeth. "Oh, I don't know, Mr. Crag. You know how hard that is."

"Mannix, you've been working under the table passing them naughty intel for months. Massage whatever contacts you have up there and get what you can on her. Something smells fishy about that dame, and if I'm going to take their case I want as much information as I can get so that I will, ideally, not wind up a pile of smoking P.I. soot on an O'Hale's barstool."

"We're taking the case after all?" Mannix said, so

excited he crushed the box of Greek candy crap to his chest. What can I say? The kid loved the job.

"I've apparently already been working it for the past twenty-four hours," I said with a sigh. "Nearly drowned twice, nearly impaled, nearly crushed by flying urinals (for the third time in my life, mind you), kidnapped, exploded, threatened by gods, sued by obese lawyers. It's hard to imagine things would get worse if I *take* the gig, and at least then you might have enough cash for one of those really topnotch pauper funeral packages they offer twice monthly over at St. Regent's Drive-Thru Cathedral. Let me have that file again, then get Miss Ravelli on the blower."

Mannix practically danced out the door and returned a moment later with not only Doris' mislabeled Ravioli file, but that morning's edition of the *Gazette*.

As he left the room once more, I flipped the file open and flicked quickly through the papers inside, hoping that I might catch by surprise some relevant fact I'd missed that morning. Nothing jumped out at me, and then I heard Mannix talking on the phone in the outer room and calling in that he had the pain in my ass herself on the horn.

"Good afternoon, Mr. Banyon," Miss Ravelli said. "I understand you've changed your mind about taking our case."

"You got that wrong, sister," I corrected. "I have had my mind changed *for* me about taking your case. It is a distinction with a very large difference. If it were up to my mind alone, it would be at this moment valiantly struggling to keep me vertical while my favorite bartender and I blasted away bits of it a la Space Invaders."

I figured she'd know I meant the old video game and

not the actual space invaders who tracked back and forth across England last October while getting picked off one by one by RAF missile defense. Limeys got nearly all of them until the last one started moving so fast it couldn't be hit. It finally landed on a cow in Lincolnshire. Turns out the alien fleet was only looking for directions to Uranus. It takes all kinds.

Anyway, space invaders didn't matter because I'd just had something a hell of a lot more important catch my eye.

Miss Ravelli was blathering on about how relieved she was that I was taking the case and hoping that it'd mean the strange phone calls would stop.

"Hold that thought, sweetheart," I said.

I dropped the receiver to my desk and fumbled around in my top drawer, pulling out a large magnifying glass.

Yeah, we actually do use magnifying glasses in the trade, just like housewives use them to check the expiration dates on coupons. But thanks to TV and movies I don't know a P.I. in the business who isn't embarrassed to have one and who doesn't stuff it in the back of a drawer … close at hand, but hidden behind something dignified like a racing form or girly magazine.

While I was talking to Poseidon's wife, I'd finally glanced at the newspaper Mannix had brought in with Mrs. Ravioli's file. The banner headline read **TO SEA OR NOT TO SEA** which, as exquisitely horrible headlines went, wasn't the worst the *Gazette* had ever come up with. (The most spectacularly awful one was **OH, SH*T!** after that manure-powered dirigible blew up all over Carter and Mondale during a whistle-stop in '80. I still don't know what the Pulitzer committee was smoking that year.)

It wasn't the irreversible tailspin in which modern journalism was lost for which I'd hauled out my magnifying glass.

Even though there hadn't been a storm in days, the coast was flooding again. Several islands were now completely underwater, and some areas near the shore were getting washed away. There was a large photograph accompanying the lead story. It was an area of town I was more familiar with than I'd have liked to be, having missed my train and being forced to hike out of it on foot the previous day.

The Seaweed Palace Bar was underwater. So was the taffy shop next door. There were people stuck up on the roofs, and I noticed among them the love-of-my-life waitress who'd launched a rotting Vincetti fish special at my innocent head.

The plight of the men and women trapped on the roof was what had interested the photographer. I was more concerned with what was in the background.

The back of the photo was a panoramic view of the opposite side of the bay. The piers were gone, completely covered by water. Some of the loose docks were breaking up and bobbing around in the churned-up foam and seaweed. Big and small boats were crashing together like it was mating season at the yacht club.

The cement stairs that led from the bay up to the back of the mall were halfway underwater. I brought the magnifying glass up and squinted at the little figure in white I thought I'd spied at the top of the steps.

Parka Man stood before the Footlocker sign, both arms raised high in the air, Poseidon's trident clutched in his right hand.

I grabbed up the phone.

"Okay, here's the deal," I informed Mrs. Poseidon. "Four grand deposited in my account right away. I'll put my elf back on the phone. He handles my finances."

"That's fine," Miss Ravelli said. "I told you, money isn't a problem."

I took another look through the magnifying glass at the bastard in the sunglasses who had tried to kill me three times and would try again as soon as he found out I was no longer lying dead on a sleazy tavern's men's room floor with a latrine lobotomy.

"In that case, six grand," I amended. "Plus expenses. You'll get an itemized bill either from me or the executor of my estate. How soon can we meet?"

"I can send a dolphin for you right away."

"Make it an hour. I have to stop by the local newspaper first. Plus that'll give you time to deposit the cash. I don't get the money upfront, I don't do the work. Remember, that's American dollars. Yes, they'll be worth less than drachmas next year, but I'm a sentimentalist. It was dollars that first got me loaded."

I called out to Mannix and transferred the call over to him to make all the arrangements.

As I put my magnifying glass back in my desk I noticed the two strands of grass skirt I'd found at two of the places Parka Man had tried to kill me. When I found them I wasn't interested in taking the case. Now that I was taking it, I didn't have time to follow down on the lead. Hopefully I'd have a chance to wrap them around the little SOB's neck and pull until his bastard eyes popped the lenses out of his Foster Grants. In fact, I'd have penciled that in for the next day, but I still didn't have a goddamn pocket calendar.

"And when you're done out there, run out and pick me up a pocket calendar!" I hollered out to Mannix, who was still on the phone with Mrs. Poseidon.

I snatched up the copy of the *Gazette*, tore the picture from the front page, took a quick glancing inventory around the office so I could remember what it looked like before the next inevitable catastrophe, got ticked anew at the parka-wearing bastard who'd trashed the joint, and hustled my keister out the door and into the waiting arms of my impending suicide.

8

I had to take a cab two miles out of the city to find a spot where the ocean wasn't attacking the beach like Kirstie Alley mauling a ten-pound Christmas ham.

Outside the city limits, the sea grew calm. Parka Man was apparently focusing all his firepower further inland. I figured now I had a pretty good idea why.

Mannix had arranged the pickup spot with Miss Ravelli. It was near the old summer camp that always did a booming business even though a machete-wielding maniac used to come to life and slaughter teenagers there every summer back in the 1980s, all because the AAA Tour Book mistakenly gave it the 3-diamond rating meant for Wild Bill's Rootin' Tootin' Campground (with pool, seasonal only) down the road.

I already don't trust dolphins because they're so playful and look like they're smiling all the time. Who doesn't want to punch one in the face? That day gave me an all-new reason to hate them: punctuality. At precisely four o'clock one of the happy little bastards rose from the water of the lagoon where I was cooling my heels on the shore.

The dolphin did a backflip that I figured was supposed to impress both me and itself. It unleashed a couple of those cheerful ack-ack noises that make a sensible human being want to strangle the big, dumb fish if only evolution had had the decency to give them the kind of necks you can wrap your fingers around. Then it swam like a rocket over to where I was standing wondering if I should just shoot it and go home.

It had a little seat behind the fin just big enough for me to squeeze into. A harness wrapped around its belly. I waded out, climbed on, and we were off in a flash.

The thing moved like lightning across the calm surface of the lagoon. The sun was out and the air had been warm onshore, but the wind that cut across my exposed face as we headed out to sea grew cold fast. The tails of my trench coat flapped like crazy, the brim of my fedora bent back, and my necktie took on a life of its own as it snaked up over my shoulder and pointed desperately to the dry land I never should have vacated.

With my peripheral vision I saw the fingers of green land that stretched out left and right quickly thin from dense trees and underbrush to hard black beach and wave-pounded rocks. The land vanished in our wake, the sky dropped, the water rose and before I could suck in a last desperate gulp of air we'd plunged completely underwater.

I hate enchanted animals and objects. They're always so smug. Doris brought back a dancing and singing British teapot once after one of her million vacations with that battleaxe mother of hers. She insisted it would cheer up the office. I almost had a heart attack when I staggered to my couch in the middle of the night and it jumped out from behind the trash bucket and started singing some goddamn song about self-improvement and good personal hygiene. After I'd quite sensibly shot the hell out of it, Doris tried to glue the pieces back together the next morning, but after that it was only ever surly and cursing, and the only song it sang was "Goldfinger." I liked the improvement. Doris didn't, especially after I put it in charge of the office whenever I wasn't there. The thing mysteriously vanished during one of my three-day O'Hale's spirits-tasting sabbaticals, and when I came back Doris insisted that it went off to find some broken teacup kid that it had left in a bag along with the register receipt on the steps of Bed, Bath & Beyond.

My dolphin taxi had been enchanted somehow as well. The air bubble that magically formed around me made unnecessary the breath that instinct wanted me to take before we ducked under the waves. Except for my shoes and pants below the knee where I'd waded out to my ride, my clothes remained perfectly dry.

Unfortunately, I was pretty dry as well. I had all that good, cheap Greek booze back at the office, but I hadn't had time to sample any of it. It was a crying shame, because now would have been an excellent time to be well and truly shitfaced.

The sea grew dark around us. I looked up and saw the rays of daylight that sliced through the water fading away like the spark of life fleeing the eyes of a bum dying alone and unloved at the back of a dank alley. When the last natural light vanished a second later, we were alone in a vast primordial darkness that was so terrifying I understood why man's ancient fish ancestor first flopped out of the sea and invented Bacardi.

My skin wasn't exposed to the numbing cold I was sure had developed outside the thin membrane of the air pocket in which I sat clinging like a maniac to the dolphin's reins. Somehow the total blackness grew even darker, and I sensed that we were moving faster. I felt it in my stomach even if I couldn't see it with my eyes.

Beats me how far we traveled. We were going through pitch darkness at dolphin warp eight, and it's not like I'd ever been invited over to the Poseidon place before for croquet and cocktails — shrimp or the good kind. I only knew we'd dropped out of supersonic speed when my stomach lurched like I'd gotten a Timberland to the gut, there was a flash of brilliant light and I was suddenly surrounded by so many sea monsters I figured the little happy bastard on whose back I was parked was getting his revenge on mankind through me for *Flipper*.

I saw almost as many crooked fangs, bulging abdomens, grotesque pasty flesh, slippery limbs and freakishly bulging eyes as I do at Kmart.

A huge tentacle covered in suction cups and as long as a downtown bus flipped up and lashed down like a whip. It moved so fast that I didn't have time to pull my piece, not that I figured a revolver would work underwater and against a monster so big it made my flabby ex-mother-in-law with the three chins and dump-truck ass look like one of those bony society dames with toothpick arms and Bizarro Maria Shriver cheekbones.

As the limb shot towards me I got a mental flash of me shooting off a round, the bubble around me piercing, and me freezing to death and gulping for air a million miles below the surface of the ocean. Either way, I was sure i was a goner.

An instant later, the weak light that was somehow brightening the underwater domain of Poseidon winked out as the monster's arm closed in for the kill.

The massive, fat limb seemed to slap some invisible barrier and slide off, leaving me and my dolphin pal unharmed. I looked back and the end of the suction cups had formed something like a fist that the frustrated beast shook at us as we sped away.

Some of the monster's pals tried to make a grab at me as well. I had every kind of flapping limb and snapping jaw you can imagine looking to make me a P.I. hors d'oeuvre. They all wound up disappointed and holding onto their giant boxes of soggy Triscuits. The invisible water tunnel the dolphin was carting me down was unbreakable.

We traveled that way for a good half-mile, down a corridor that was impervious to every attempt by the sea monsters outside to penetrate it. They grabbed, they bit, they let loose with impotent roars that were muffled by the barrier and the oxygen bubble that surrounded me, but we rode right past all of them.

Once the initial scared shitlessness passed and I figured out I wasn't going to be enjoying my golden years clinging for dear life to a sea monster's colon and hoping like hell it didn't get its slippery mitts on a giant bran muffin, I took a look around. I realized I could only see the dark shadows of the monsters all around me because of the light that rose from the sea floor up ahead. It began as a dull white glow, but became more intense as we approached. The number of sea monsters thinned the closer we got to it.

We had voyaged to the bottom of the sea, and the natural landscape illuminated by the artificial light was boring and flat, like traveling all the way to the end of the world only to find Mary Steenburgen. Aside from the odd giant squid that floated past giving us the finger from multiple tentacles, there was pretty much nothing down there but a series of dark hills and a lot of featureless nothingness.

I did catch sight of something below us as we passed over it. Beneath the silt peeked out bits of bronze that I at first thought were pieces of some larger object that had been broken and scattered on the ocean floor. I only caught sight of the larger shape of the items as we were leaving it behind, and when I quickly glanced in either direction I realized the small, shiny bits were just the visible fragments of a single large object. It was huge and was most likely circular, since it arced off in either direction and vanished along a massive curve in the distance both ways. The area that the gigantic hula hoop encircled had to cover miles.

The dolphin pulled low to the floor and once we'd passed beyond the shiny metal, the ocean melted away around us and we were back in open air.

It was like passing from a cave behind a waterfall and back into the sunlight. There was a river that led into a lagoon, and the dolphin swam right up into the bay and stopped at a dock, acking like a madman and nodding for me to get the hell off.

The oxygen pocket melted from around me as I dismounted onto the dock.

There were other dolphins wearing harnesses playing with a plastic bowling pin in what I figured was some kind of sea mammal parking lot, and my ride took off to bat the stupid little toy around with his blow-holed confreres.

I thought I'd felt my shoes and legs dry out as we passed through the barrier into Poseidon's realm, and sure enough my socks didn't squish as I took a little step to check them out on the solid surface of the gleaming white dock.

"Welcome to our humble home, Mr. Banyon," a dame's voice called, and I glanced up from my fascinating shoes to find Miss Ravelli standing in an archway decked out in a seaweed and samite dressing gown.

Poseidon's humble home was an undersea palace of marble that sparkled so brilliantly it was as if there was a light bulb tucked away inside every massive slab. The soaring parapets sparkled with light from a source I couldn't see.

Now that I was in it, I was sure that the hole in the ocean was a couple of miles across. It was like standing at the bottom of a huge well. A towering ring of water walls rose up on all sides. When I looked up, the vast distance made it look like the tunnel narrowed to a virtual pinprick. Far, far up above was an open circle to the top of the sea and the rest of the world. I could barely see a tiny patch of what I could only assume from that distance was blue sky and yellow sunlight.

"Impressive, isn't it?" Miss Ravelli asked. "I couldn't believe it the first time Poseidon took me down here, me being a human being who was born on dry land and all. I bet you've never seen anything like it."

"I have, in point of fact, seen something exactly like it just this morning. That ring I just saw buried in the silt outside has 'made on Olympus' stamped all over it. In fact, give me a broom and a bathysphere and I can probably find the patent mark. I saw one just like it in a goldfish bowl in the general store of an exhibitionist god who can apparently figure out how to make everything except something to keep his sheet up."

"You were on Olympus?" Miss Ravelli asked, confusion and concern on her face. "You didn't tell me that on the phone."

"Sister, you don't know the half of what I didn't tell you. C'mon, let's get inside. I don't like the way my dolphin chauffeur is grinning and slapping his fin at me and, much like Vulcan, I'm in desperate need of a belt."

9

The archway at the end of the marble dock led through a high wall. On the other side was a miles-wide expanse filled with gleaming marble buildings, sprawling lawns, farmland, roads and orchards. Poseidon had brought an entire city with him when he'd moved down from the surface of the ancient world.

A sign pounded into a grass-lined road that led down from the palace to the city read, "Water World, pop. 45,982." The bucolic undersea setting seemed a hell of a lot less horrible than the shitty movie that I figured swiped its name.

I had no idea if the people were all descended from ancient Greeks or if there had been fresh stock brought down throughout the millennia. The people were dots in the distance, riding around in chariots, tilling the fields, scrubbing the marble, probably molesting the hell out of the resident ovines, and by and large being the subservient opposite of the mob of entitled pedophiles I'd seen ringing Olympus screaming for blood and treasure, but willing to settle for treasure plus an all-expense paid, catamite-catered luxury Aegean resort vacation for eleven million, plus guests.

Nearby, Poseidon's palace really was the only joint in town fit for a god and his 100-meter Olympic swimming silver-medallist trophy wife with the big cans. Lots of marble, towers capped with gold. The whole fairy tale schmear.

"Looks like you and Poseidon are doing all right for yourselves," I said as she led me through a side door and into a gold-lined hallway.

"Salvage is very lucrative," Miss Ravelli said. "Poseidon comes back with treasure a couple of times a week, and there's still an untapped fortune out there at the bottom of the sea." She shot me a hairy eyeball. "I signed a prenup, Mr. Banyon, if that's what you're thinking. I'm not interested in my husband's money."

"Then go stand on the other side of the gymnasium with the asthmatic wallflowers, because you're the only one I've met at the dance today who isn't."

I could see she was a dame who didn't like being confused. There was angry frustration under her fresh look of perplexity, and it wore on her about as well as last year's braces and training bra on this year's prom queen.

She took me to the kitchen and offered me a drink that looked like she'd fished the ingredients from the clogged garbage disposal. When I refused, she kept it for herself and we sat at the kitchen table while I laid it all out for her.

"Where's Poseidon?" I asked. "I only like to repeat myself when I'm ordering rounds of liquid appetizers at my favorite speakeasy."

"He's at work," she said. "He should be home soon. Who wants my husband's money? And what were you doing on Olympus?"

I told her all about Mercury showing up twice at my office, my fun-filled abduction, the threats from Zeus, and Vulcan's oblivious admission that the entire population of Olympus was in the process of Anatevka-ing its way the hell out of Greece.

"Well, they…they can't possibly think they're moving here," she said.

As I spilled it all out for her, I kept a close eye on her. Her face paled like a sheet, and I've peddled around the block enough times to know that even Julius and Ethel Rosenberg's ghosts couldn't fake shock that good. This was all news to her.

Despite her evident astonishment, she never released her drink. She just kept right on sucking down the glass of brown goo.

"They are clearly under the impression that they *are* moving in," I corrected. "By Tuesday, specifically. Are you going to keep drinking that?"

She hadn't realized she was still sipping from her glass. She held it away, surprised it was in her hand, and sighed. "One's body is a temple, Mr. Banyon."

"Mine's ecumenical, sweetheart. It embraces all proofs, from happy hour through closing time, no ID required." I reached into my trench coat pocket and slapped a picture down in the middle of the table.

I'd stopped by the *Gazette* before I'd left town to get a better photo of the SOB with the trident who was smashing the hell out of all the taffy shops on the east side of town. The picture in the paper had been grainy, and the parka-wearing asshole was barely visible in the distance. I'd had a buddy at the paper digitally enlarge that section of the original photo they had on file and then run out a picture of Parka Man's face. All it cost me was the promise of a bottle of fine, imported cheap Greek booze. Everybody's a goddamn humanitarian.

"You ever seen this slob before?" I asked.

The image wasn't great, but it was better than the view any of us had had at the health bar the previous morning. She picked up the picture and studied Parka Man's nose, mouth, chin and cheeks.

"Well, I know he's the same man from The Seaweed Palace Bar," she said, "but I don't recognize his face."

"He never did any work around the joint?" I asked. "I don't just mean regular servants. People always forget electricians, cable guys, plumbers. You have any contractors in grass skirts doing work the past couple of weeks?"

"No, I'm sorry. You can ask Poseidon. Maybe he worked here before we were married. I know he had a new roof put on a few years ago. And Sodomite & Son replaced the *puer delicatus* in the andronitis a couple of times. That's it as far as I know."

Turns out I didn't have to wait to question the bleached-blond nitwit himself, since at that moment Poseidon came stomping into the kitchen hauling two giant crates propped up one to each massive shoulder.

"Hey, babe, I'm home."

The god of the sea caught one look at me sitting at the table and his wife sitting all nervous-like across from me, and dropped the crates to the floor. Turns out they were old rotting wooden chests, and when they hit the marble floor they split open and spilled two giant piles of gold coins as well as necklaces, tiaras and gold and silver goblets all the way over to the Whirlpool fridge and the cellar stairs.

"What are *you* doing here?" Poseidon demanded.

"I'll give you three guesses, I.Q., and the first two don't have anything to do with buggering fish."

"I hired him, honey," Miss Ravelli interjected, jumping to her feet and grabbing onto and massaging one of her husband's giant, tan forearms. "I tried to call you."

"Phone cracked again," Poseidon said with a grunt. He tossed on the table a cell phone that had snapped in the ocean's great depths. "They work for shit under pressure."

"Your phone and I are kindred spirits," I suggested.

"Yeah, yeah, Banyon. I don't like you or your smart mouth."

"Merely an understandable natural instinct to recoil from that which accurately contrasts your inherent obtuseness," I said, with a big, fat, disarming smile plastered across my kisser. "That's me apologizing for any misunderstanding."

The wife got it. Lucky for me, the moron didn't.

"Yeah, all right," Poseidon said, kicking through the coins and joining his wife at the kitchen table across from me. "So what can you do about the phone calls and mail?"

"Well, I'd actually like you to pack up the mail and get it to my office."

She immediately got on the kitchen phone and made a call. The dame was efficient. She ordered the Water World undersea post office to bag up everything and send it to my office pronto. She was back at the table in less than a minute.

"The Postmaster Admiral will have it shipped out by

whale mail within the hour," she assured me. "I hope it will help, Mr. Banyon."

"Hopefully hope isn't all we've got to go on," I told her. "There might be something in there we can find to track this guy down."

I tapped the photo of Parka Man on the table. Poseidon tipped his head to take a look at the close-up picture.

"What does Makalooka have to do with this?" Poseidon asked.

He realized he'd said something important when his wife and I both shot him one of those over-the-top, cartoon-reaction glances.

"You know him, honey?" Miss Ravelli pressed.

"Well, yeah. Sure I do," Poseidon said cautiously. "He hooked up the DirecTV dish on the roof two weeks ago. It was when you were at your sister's those two days."

She shook her head. "We haven't been hooked up," she insisted. "Wood's Hole said it would take months to lower down the van."

"What do you know about this guy?" I demanded.

Poseidon clearly didn't like being in the hot seat. If it was just me pressuring him he'd have probably just whipped up a monsoon as a distraction and ducked out the pantry door. But the wife was giving him a look too, and I could see the god of the sea really had something good going with this dame.

"I don't know," Poseidon said. "He was just some island native, I guess. I'm not racist," he added quickly. "It's just I've swamped so many islands...*allegedly*. Most of those were done by Zeus and Vulcan. Tectonic plates and volcanoes."

"Yeah, you gave me that whole song and dance yesterday," I said. "Don't sweat it. It's almost impossible to lift a fingerprint from a tsunami."

"Right," Poseidon said. "Well, I still don't know what to tell you. He had a grass skirt and a DirecTV jacket when he came to the door. I just let him in. I was in a hurry that day. You were gone, hon, and I had to fix my own breakfast. I burned the toast."

"That's fascinating," I informed him. "Hold on, because if there was jelly involved I'm going to want to take copious notes."

"Shut up, Banyon," Poseidon said. "Anyway, I burned the toast because the toaster was set too high. You always set it too high," he told the little woman. "Makalooka went upstairs. He said he could access the roof from the rampart outside our bedroom. I had that hurricane I'd been working on in the mid-Atlantic, so I was in a hurry and I left. I got halfway to the subtropical ridge when I realized I forgot my trident at home, and I had to turn the dolphins around and come all the way back. That's the first time I noticed it was gone."

"So was the satellite guy," I pointed out.

"Don't say it like that, Banyon," Poseidon snarled. "He was just the cable guy. I didn't figure anything was wrong. I figured he'd gone back to a ship on the surface to get a pair of pliers or something. I turned the place upside-down for days looking for my trident — we both did — and by the time we were sure it was gone I guess Makalooka just kind of slipped my mind. I mean, who remembers the cable guy?"

"Satellite," I corrected. "And he wasn't that either."

"Whatever," the god of the sea said. "I just wanted the Weather Channel. The antenna on the tower has been worthless ever since the switchover to digital."

I leaned back in my chair. "Well, it could be worse. At least we still know next to nothing about the guy your brother hired to come in and swipe your trident, so your total knowledge vacuum didn't actually suck what little we knew from our brains."

"Wait, what? What about my brother?"

I gave him the short version of what I'd learned from my trip to Mount Olympus. I made sure I used the smallest possible words which I figured was still a long-shot, but had the greatest chance of sticking to the inferior frontal gyrus of his moron brain.

I knew he'd gotten it when he jumped to his feet, swirling storm clouds forming in the irises of his outraged eyes.

I figured from the muffled booms, the shaking appliance, and the water suddenly running out the front door that some bottles of Evian in the fridge had just exploded. The pipes in the cupboard under the sink groaned like a son of a bitch.

"Dear, the plumbing," Miss Ravelli warned, eyeballing her growling Kohler.

But this time a little rub to the arm wasn't enough to keep the god of the sea from going typhoon on somebody's ass. Even without his trident, it was obvious that water anywhere in his immediate vicinity needed to sweat like bottles of Stolichnaya when they get a whiff of my thirsty liver.

"Zeus! No way! That is bulfinch! There is no way he's moving down here!"

"He can't," I explained. "Not while you're here."

"Damn straight!" Poseidon hollered.

"Your brother's getting desperate," I said. "That's why this bastard's doing what he's doing right now." I tapped a finger to the picture of the phony DirecTV guy in the parka.

"What the hell does *he* have to do with all this?" Poseidon demanded.

"Mr. Banyon says he's waiting for you near the health bar we were at yesterday," his goddamn helpful wife stupidly interjected.

That was all the angry god needed. He charged for the door.

I made the mistake of trying to get out in front of him, and the next thing I knew I was getting a solid arm like a block of granite to the chest, and I was flying back across the kitchen. The door of the stainless steel Whirlpool fridge collapsed under my weight, the back of my head snapped back and I saw a flash of light.

The last image I saw was Poseidon charging like an enraged bull out the kitchen door, the wife crying and pleading with him and running out behind him.

Somehow through the growing cloudy haze I realized I was sitting in a puddle of water for the millionth time in the past twenty-four hours, but before I could utter so much as a single appropriate curse of complaint about my goddamn sopping wet ass, the lights winked out and the whole kitchen went dark.

10

I was out like a light for I don't know how long. When I came to I was seeing stars and I felt something hard whacking me repeatedly on top of the head.

When I'd dented the front of the fridge door, I'd started the ice machine. Cube after cube was smacking me on my skull. Judging by the skating rink the floor around me had become, I'd been out for a good five minutes. There was a ton of ice mixed in with the pile of gold coins Poseidon had dumped out on the floor.

I was hauling my bruised carcass off the wet tile when Miss Ravelli came running back into the room, red-eyed and frantic.

"He's gone!" the dame wailed. "He got in his chariot and took off. I'm afraid he's going to do something stupid, Mr. Banyon."

"I would've figured you'd be used to that by now," I said. "You know, your husband being a complete moron and all."

I touched my elbow and winced. I thought I must have whacked it a third time, but I wasn't sure. All I knew was that it hurt like hell, pretty much like every other square inch of me. I took one step, slipped on a cube of ice and fell right back to my ass.

"That's it," I said. "Take back the money. I quit."

"Mr. Banyon, *please*," she begged. "He's going to try to get his trident back."

I kept my rear end planted in the puddle on the floor, ice cubes hammering me in the noggin.

"That is unadvisable," I said. "I pretty much figure that's been Zeus' plan all along. The other gods have been cooking this up for a hundred years. The Greek economy collapsing is just dumb coincidental timing that's giving them cover. They were leaving Olympus anyway. Your husband is a hothead. Everybody knows it. They shoved that iceberg out in front of the Titanic and then blamed him for it. To supposedly keep peace with the Leprechaun Mob they fitted him with that ankle monitor that kept him off dry land. But he was never supposed to stay in the water for a whole century. They were sure he'd lose his cool and step on shore and boom. But the hothead shocked every bastard god on Olympus and actually managed to hold on all this time. The clock was ticking, time was running out. The monitor was coming off in a couple of weeks. So Zeus had to push the issue by getting somebody to steal your husband's trident and start playing around with the seas. That's all that asshole in the parka's purpose in all this has been: to lure your husband onto shore. I don't know his motivation in all this…maybe it's personal or maybe he was just paid off. But he's the one who planted the seahorse head in your bed, he's been making the hang-up calls and sending the threatening notes to wire you people up real good. Of course, if he hadn't gone all WWF and flattened me unconscious against this heavy appliance, I would have told your idiot husband all this."

If I had any residual doubt of the dame's intentions, I lost them then as I laid it out for her. Her face grew more horrified with each word, until she was so completely terrified for her husband that the tears dried up before the waterworks could even start full blast, and all I was left with hovering over me was a frantic woman whose only concern was for her dumb spouse's stupid neck.

"Mr. Banyon, you *can't* let him do this," she insisted.

"And yet here I sit getting clocked on the head with ice cubes. Say, this is a lot of ice for one fridge, isn't it? How much does one of these numbers set you back?"

She waded furiously through the ice and gold coins, grabbed me by the lapels of my trench coat and with a mighty wrench tried hauling me up off the floor. All she managed was to slide me across the water puddle and knock me sideways so that I whacked my elbow for the fourth time, this time on the marble tile floor.

"Knock it off, lady! All right already."

I slipped and stumbled and somehow made it across the floor, which was pretty much like every late afternoon except the usual path to my loss of equilibrium was generally a hell of a lot more enjoyable. I scooped up my fedora from the table and the two of us made our way back outside the palace.

We took off at a sprint down the path to the wall that led to the lagoon and the dolphin parking lot.

I saw trouble the instant we ran through the archway.

There was a dame standing down at the far end of the pier. She held some hunk of triangular metal in her hand

and was aiming it at the sheer wall of water that separated Poseidon's kingdom from the deepest, nastiest depths of the sea.

"What the hell is she doing here?" I demanded as we ran.

"She's just an itinerant muse," Miss Ravelli explained. "She showed up at the door this morning offering to inspire me to write a better shopping list for the grocery store. I'm always forgetting the bananas when I get to Kroger's. *Hurry*, Mr. Banyon."

I hurried all right. I hurried up and pulled my piece from its holster.

"Hold it right there, sister!" I hollered.

The dame looked back with a start and shot me the same spiteful, strung-out look I'd seen once already that day. She was the same big-mouthed muse I'd seen screaming bloody murder at Mercury on the steps of Zeus' temple back on Olympus.

She wheeled back to the wall of water and aimed the metal doohickey in her hand like she was Commissioner Gordon pointing the goddamn Bat-Signal.

The vertical face of water sat beyond the short stretch of river at the end of the small lagoon. It was like one of those undersea viewing areas they have at the aquarium, where grammar school kids get to flip-off whales swimming by the glass.

In this case there weren't any whales in sight, probably because they'd been swallowed whole by any number of the colossal monsters that had been slowly circling Poseidon's home, drooling into their own reeking wakes and looking for a doorway into the human buffet that was the city of Water World for the past few thousand years.

Unlike the aquarium, it wasn't comforting thick glass separating us from the bulging eyes and hungry stomachs on the other side, but some kind of divine hoodoo.

Whatever Olympian technology Vulcan had built into the huge ring half-buried in the silt outside, it was not impervious to the device he'd hammered together and given to the babe in the bed sheets at the end of the dock. She aimed, the wall of water that was keeping the ocean from coming in started shimmering, and the next thing I knew something dark and fast was being vomited out the now-permeable sheer water face.

When you're looking at a wall of water seven miles high, even Everest is going to look like a midget on his knees in comparison. With that monster wall as a backdrop, the real monsters that were suddenly rampaging across the grass beside the lagoon looked tiny. It was only as they closed in that I realized how big they really were.

The first had been followed by a second, then a third.

They were some kind of deep-sea shark-headed man-monsters. Huge heads, massive dorsal fins, but with bodies built like Schwarzenegger in his prime. They'd had eyes at some point in their history, but the ocean's depths had turned them milky white and covered them with a thin film like cobwebs. They apparently made up for a lack of eyes with nostrils that'd make a truffle hog jealous. The trio barely sniffed the air once before making a beeline directly for me, Miss Ravelli, and the idiot muse at the end of the dock who was so strung out she had no idea she was ringing a dinner gong.

I slammed on the brakes halfway down the dock, and Miss Ravelli plowed into me, then tried to shove her way past.

"Ignore them!" she shouted, as I held her back. "We have to help my husband!"

"I'm sure you must have a very good idea how us being lunch will help but, regrettably, I'm ashamed to admit I'm at a goddamn loss."

A bunch of dolphins were still dolled up in harnesses and saddles in the lagoon, but the playful bastards weren't as dumb as their idiot grins and crazy cackling suggested. When the shark-headed freaks flew down the grassy slope, through the thick cattails that rimmed the lagoon, and started splashing across the shallow water's edge, the five brave dolphins immediately booked it for the other side of the pond, acking like a society dame who'd just had a mouse slipped down the back of her swanky evening gown.

I'm a pretty good shot, especially when I'm sober which, unfortunately, I was disgustingly so at that moment. I figured I'd take out the hunk of metal in the muse's hands easy, then hightail it back for cover until we could figure out what to do about the couple of monsters who'd managed to sneak in the barn while the hayloft was open. Too bad my tactical brilliance hadn't taken into account how fast the shark-heads might be.

Once they hit the water of the lagoon, they were like ICBMs. The trio zipped to the marble pier and the first one was up and running on stumpy legs before I'd manage to get a bead on the triangular piece of metal in the dame's hands.

Their leader ran across the pier to the dock that stuck

off the end, where at that moment the suddenly screaming and horrified muse was probably musing some amusing ode to mortality. Too bad for her she didn't have a pen and paper to jot her thoughts down real quick before the racing shark tipped his head, snapped his massive jaws, and split her into two impressively equal halves.

The object in her hands flew up in the air in a wide arc. I just missed seeing it splash down in the middle of the lagoon because at that moment the next two shark-heads leaped up onto the pier five yards away from me and Miss Ravelli.

They had teeth like snapping bear traps. I could see the rotting flesh of whatever luckless bastard had been their last meal clinging to their razor-sharp choppers. The veils of cobwebs over their eyes were like miniature shrouds, covering crystal balls in which swirled sightless white mist. They were ugly as a son of a bitch, with blue leather heads and flaring nostrils so big they could pick two-fisted all day and never shake hands with themselves. Their bodybuilder physiques were impressive, but they'd neglected the sunlamp. Their skin was paler than a Swedish stewardess' ass.

They stopped, cut loose with an impressive roar like a couple of undersea lions, which I guess was supposed to scare the shit out of us. It probably worked with plankton, but it stupidly gave me the time I needed to shoot one of the bastards in the head.

The slug slapped the shark-headed monster on the right dead center in the wide area between his pair of bugging, blind eyes. The monster went down like a drunk Swedish stewardess in a cheap motel, smearing the marble with a streak of ugly blood.

The remaining nearer one let out another roar, but this time it did so while charging straight at us. The one at the end of the dock got the message. It left its half-eaten muse and raced with its pal for the spot where me and old lady Poseidon stood with an invisible flashing neon "come and get it" sign dangling over our heads.

If I'd had time, I would have pegged at least one more, but the SOBs moved too fast. Before I could get a bead on one, they were both on us.

I get a lot of luck in my sad-sack life, but rarely the good kind. As I shoved Mrs. Poseidon behind me and prepared for a close quarters shootout that'd no doubt end in two seconds flat with me as the main slab of liverwurst in a submarine sandwich fit for a shark, I somehow managed something that almost never happened in a life of bum luck and sinking in the shit stream rapids without a life preserver: I drew four aces.

In the split-second between launching themselves at us and actually reaching us, the pair of briny bastards got a funny look on both their monster faces. It happened so fast I couldn't believe the rapid change in expressions. It was like a Swedish stewardess when you told her the next day that you were broke and she was going to have to pay for the room. (Hey, sue me for beating a metaphor within an inch of its life. I had a kidnapped will o' the wisp case in Stockholm last year.) The sharks went from kings of the deep to mewling shrimp. They slid to a stop on their pasty, slimy feet, took a couple of big snorts at the air, then turned right around and ran off back where they came from.

They jumped over the body of their dead pal and kept right on going, zipping back across the water at top speed, zooming up through the weeds, running at a full sprint across the grass and plowing right back through the vertical wall of water.

From their first appearance to the moment they vanished back into the brackish deep took all of thirty seconds.

There was a kind of wobbly fuzziness to the wall where they disappeared, and I could see reflected in the dark water the shimmering shape of a massive triangle. The gizmo the muse had aimed at the wall was still up and running, even at the bottom of the pond. I thought about the similar item I'd picked up back at Vulcan's gift shop.

When the volcano god had pulled that one out of the fishbowl on Olympus, the water flowed into the vacant spot in the bowl. Replacing it had reopened the water tunnel up the middle of the fishbowl. That thing in his shop had operated like an on/off switch, so maybe just smashing the triangle would put out of commission whatever Olympian magic had opened the portal in the water wall. Unfortunately I was going to have a hard time finding it in the mud somewhere out in the middle of the lagoon.

I figured I was going for yet another swim, but I didn't even have a chance to yank off my shoes.

The shark-headed bastards had barely run back out the open triangular door when something infinitely more bladder-voiding entered stage right.

The head came through first. It was as big as a Volkswagen Beetle, with stringy black strands of mottled hair, bulging, bloodshot eyes, and three mouths lined with vicious rows of razor sharp fangs. When the second head came through I figured the babe had an uglier sister until I realized the pair of scaly giraffe-like necks were attached to the same misshapen torso. By the third and fourth heads I'd all but given up hope of making it back to O'Hale's for that evening's inaugural bag of fresh pretzels.

The parade finally stopped at a six-pack. The deep-sea Dionne quintuplets-plus one let out a chorus of roars from its eighteen different mouths and once it finished its impressive solo harmonizing, it swung all twelve monstrous eyes in our direction.

"Quick point. I did already tender my resignation, correct?" I asked Miss Ravelli.

The dame was standing behind me on the pier, gripping my biceps like she was squeezing orange juice by hand and staring up at the looming creature that was still in the process of slithering its way through the portal in the water wall. It had about a dozen giant tentacle legs, what looked like a huge cat's tail, and as an added bonus in the #1 Freaks of the Deep category, a belt of barking dog's heads encircled her waist.

"Her name's Scylla," Miss Ravelli explained, terrified eyes trained at the topmost head that towered three stories above the ground and glared malevolently down at the current wife of the king of the sea. "She and my husband used to go together back when they were in high school. She never got over him. She's been down here circling for centuries. He even got a restraining order a few years ago, but as long as she was out there, she was a hundred yards away and so the cops couldn't do anything."

I wished I had a phone on me to call 911, because Scylla was clearly in O.J. mode as the last of her slimy tentacles slipped through the shimmering wall and slapped so hard on the ground that I felt the shockwaves under my shoes.

As Poseidon's old squeeze was making her dramatic slow-motion appearance, the dolphins in the lagoon were acking up a furious storm. I would have ignored them in favor of turning tail and running for all I was worth if one of them hadn't at that moment flapped a flipper and doused me like a tourist sitting in the first three rows at Sea World.

"If you hadn't noticed, you little fish bastard, I am armed, cornered, and have nothing to lose by fitting you up with a matching blowhole."

I peeled my eyes away from the looming monster.

The dolphin had its nose up on the pier. Stuck on the end was the triangular hunk of metal the muse had used to open the shimmering portal in the wall.

The multiple heads across the lagoon roared again, and I got a whiff of hot breath from six mouths that could have used about a gallon of Lavoris each.

The archway was too far away for us to reach, but it was the only option. I snatched the hunk of metal from the helpful dolphin's nose, snapped it in half, watched the flickering triangular portal in the wall twinkle brightly once then vanish, then offered Miss Ravelli the only sensible course of action open to us at that particular juncture.

"Run!" I bravely hollered.

It was every man for himself, and I had no clue if Miss Ravelli was keeping up as I flew like chivalrous goddamn Sir Lancelot down the marble pier for the archway to the palace grounds, which suddenly seemed like it was a million miles away.

I knew she'd gotten the message when we were almost to the arch and she sprinted past me on her pair of madly pumping stems. She vanished inside.

I was running full out but thanks to years of dissolute living I wasn't exactly in Olympic athlete shape, unless there's a category for the much more fun kind of shot-putting that nobody told me about. I huffed and puffed to catch up.

A shadow loomed above me, darkening the wall, the ground and probably the back of my Fruit of the Looms.

Somewhere close behind me I heard the splash of water and I figured stampeding Scylla, Poseidon's jilted girlfriend, had reached the lagoon. I knew I'd figured right when a wall of displaced water crashed over me, flooding the walkway and nearly knocking me over into the weeds that sprouted up from the mud alongside the path.

The ground shook. Mortar launched from between the massive slabs of marble as huge bricks that hadn't been disturbed in thousands of years jumped and settled with every drop of one of the behemoth broad's massive tentacles.

I don't know how I knew she'd launched a head down at me. Maybe I saw the shadow on the wall, maybe I felt the displaced air at my back. I only knew that I was suddenly instinctively diving for my belly for the open archway, and for a change it was on purpose and wasn't because I'd been tripped, tossed or loaded.

The head flashed over me and I twisted as I fell. Three rows of choppers flew by, and the last one nicked the sleeve of my trench coat. Lucky for me the tip didn't catch the fabric and it only slid along and hopped off the cuff.

The forward momentum kept the head going right past me, and it slammed hard into the marble wall. The massive noggin punched through six marble slabs, and they thundered through the other side of the wall, crashing into the interior courtyard.

The water that had sloshed up over the walkway slicked the surface, and when I landed on my busted elbow for the hundredth time in the past day, I managed to slide straight through the opening on my side, twisted, then rolled over onto my back so that by the time I slid to a stop I was prone and looking back through the open archway.

I saw a huge, scaly belly, one barking dog head from the dame's belt, and only two of the gigantic tentacles that were propelling her hard into the marble wall.

There was a crash like the end of the world. Every five-ton brick that comprised the wall rattled. A dozen nearly shook loose, and barely managed to hang precariously in place in various spots around the wall. The dog's head and tentacles backed up from the opening and lunged forward, and the wall shook mightily once more.

Two slabs of hanging marble came loose and plummeted to the ground. Their weight was so great that they didn't bounce. They just did the vertical plunge and sank halfway in the grass, like bricks dropped into Marshmallow Fluff.

The groggy head that had bashed the hole through the wall was still sticking through onto my side of the wall. Scylla's head #6 was disoriented, and I didn't blame it. Slamming your brainpan through a solid marble wall is probably one of the best ways a sea monster maniac can get a concussion, and I might have held a couple of fingers up and asked her to count if at that moment the monster dame's nearby head hadn't suddenly got its bearings, spotted me sitting on my ass on the ground, reared back and plunged her three rows of slavering choppers for my delicious chest.

Too bad for her the rest of her body chose that moment to pull away from the other side of the wall to begin another attack. She nearly snagged me but was suddenly yanked back when the slippery tentacles on the other side of the archway splattered their hideous, flapping way in reverse.

I rolled to a sitting position and glanced back. I saw Miss Ravelli hiding back in the doorway of the palace and waving me to get the hell off my ass and run inside.

I suddenly realized that I still had my piece in my hand, and before I took off like a little sissy girl I figured I owed this monster chick one good shot. Not that she'd feel it, but it'd preserve some small scrap of masculinity as I hid out in the palace root cellar and waited for undersea animal control to toss a net over the rampaging dame.

Scylla's belly was wide open. The pasty, tubby gut rippled as she readied for another charge. This one would bring the whole wall crashing down. To my left, the snarling mouths of the one head that had already made it through to my side drooled frothy spit and waited for its body to give its neck enough slack to lunge in for the kill.

As the creature reared back a final time, I took careful

aim through the door to the vast chest above her fat stomach and squeezed off a single shot.

My roscoe has served me well in some pretty tight jams over the years. There was only one time it really failed me, but at that moment in Poseidon's undersea kingdom I finally forgave it for jamming that time my ex-mother-in-law came for Thanksgiving.

I figured the bullet hit the monster in the spot just above her belly where her sternum should have been. There was probably a heart in there somewhere, since it was still broken over something Poseidon had done three thousand years ago.

I never saw the slug penetrate. There was a flash of light, a crack of thunder, and I was suddenly launching back on the leading edge of a gale force wind and slamming the back of my head on the marble path.

At least this time I didn't get knocked out. I scrambled up to my feet only to see nothing of the immediate landscape but a wash of white.

The flash from whatever had exploded had temporarily blinded me, and as my eyes cleared I stumbled back from where I figured Scylla's closest head was lunging at me with three mouths full of angry, potentially expensive dental work that'd pay off all the patients currently suing Myron Wasserbaum, D.D.S. if only the weasel dentist could figure out a way to get a three-story tall, slimy sea monster up in the elevator and cram her in his powder blue faux vinyl office chair.

"*How did you do that?*"

Miss Ravelli's voice was right at my shoulder. The dame grabbed my bashed-up elbow, I guess thinking she was helping me to my feet but only succeeding in shooting enough pain through my arm and up into my brain to abruptly clear up my fuzzy eyes.

The wall was still standing, although it looked like a pile of teetering kid's blocks that might come down any second and crush us both under a giant Q. Through the crooked archway I saw a pile of smoking remains. Nearby, Scylla's neck had mostly been yanked back through the hole in the wall, and the one head that had made it through hung slack, eyes closed and a couple of tongues lolling from a couple of mouths.

Miss Ravelli kept close behind as I stepped cautiously over to the archway and took a very careful peek outside.

The sea monster was dead. Her torso looked like it had been completely vaporized. At least I couldn't see any of it lying around the ground. I only counted two more heads and four tentacles. The heads were dead like the one on the other side of the wall, and the last life was flicking out of the tips of the tentacles as we walked around the chunks of scaly meat that garnished the path to the lagoon.

"I'd say your husband's greedy family has been hoist on its own petard, assuming a petard is a bullet made by an asshole naked gift shop-running volcano god who doesn't know enough not to stick a thunderbolt inside a .44 slug."

The danger had passed and the dolphins were queuing up at the far end of the pier. Miss Ravelli was suddenly no longer interested in the chunks of her husband's dead ex-girlfriend glistening and oozing on her front stoop. The sea god's wife charged right on past me and the gelatinous byproducts of my terrific act of heroism.

"Hurry, Mr. Banyon! We have to stop my husband before he kills himself."

Someday somebody's going to give me a heart attack by taking two seconds to appreciate me. But until that miracle day arrived, I holstered my piece and ran like hell after Miss Ravelli for the dock at the end of the pier and the waiting dolphins.

11

"Harrowing" isn't something that generally trips lightly off my pickled tongue. It's right up there with "dilettante," "sommelier," and "I'll pay the check." But the ride back home harrowed the hell out of harrowing, times about a hundred more harrows and a couple of scared shitlesses tossed in for good measure.

Miss Ravelli was like an underwater Buffalo Bill, spurring her dolphin on to speeds that buried the needle on the magical enchantment that already gave them the ability to travel from the depths of the sea to any beach on Earth in nothing flat.

My dophin wasn't about to be outdone, so even though I tried riding it like a plow horse, it rocketed along like Secretariat with his tail on fire.

We broke the surface further along the coast from the spot where I'd met my dolphin ride just a couple of hours before. The daylight was dying, and we arced so high into the air I was afraid at the apex that I'd fall off my flying fish.

The dolphin leveled off in midair and shot straight into the surface of the water, zooming along like a gray torpedo just below the waves.

The water was choppy, and white caps broke against my chest as I held onto the slick reins for dear life.

Miss Ravelli took point and raced through the water like she owned the joint. Despite my best efforts to kill the will of my dolphin by yanking back the reins and screaming at the top of my lungs, my damned fish kept pace with hers.

Poseidon's team of dolphins apparently had a harder time with the heavy chariot and steroid-pumped god they were forced to haul along behind them. Despite my latest adventure in unconsciousness back in the Poseidons' kitchen, as well as the unpleasant impediment of nearly getting eaten, I caught sight of the sea god flying into the harbor up ahead. His wife saw him too. She ground her heels harder into the sides of her dolphin and it took off even faster. I nearly fell out of my seat for the hundredth time when my dolphin broke into a flipper-fueled sprint to keep up.

The surface of the harbor was awash in broken boat pieces and chunks of dock. I saw the back deck of The Seaweed Palace Bar had been ripped off. All that remained was a couple of pilons and the undying dream that they one day would once again sell shitty drinks to rich health nuts with dead taste buds impervious to common sense.

Inside the harbor, the waves were rising and crashing like spurts from the blow holes of invisible whales. A fountain launched up next to me and my dolphin and I were tossed to one side into a pile of floating fiberglass boat scraps.

I'd twisted to one side and had just managed to haul myself back up in the saddle when I caught a glimpse of the bastard in the white parka at the top of the long staircase that led up from the harbor. He was standing near the Radio Shack sign and held his stolen trident up like Lady Liberty inviting every sorry-ass sob story into my wallet.

Another fountain of water rose like a bomb going off beside me, and through the spout and the crashing foam I caught sight of Poseidon.

The sea god was no slouch in the water sports department even without his trident. He'd stopped his chariot near the flooded landing at the bottom of the staircase and held out both arms, sweeping them together and clapping both hands.

The water on either side of him responded by rising up like twin serpents, intertwining above his head, and rocketing up towards the Radio Shack loading dock.

Parka Man intercepted with the trident. He caught the water a dozen feet before it even reached him, and with one sweep of the three-pronged sea fork redirected the deadly missile of water out over the harbor where it burst apart and fell like harmless rain.

That his own weapon had been used against him evidently infuriated Poseidon. I heard the god bellow a deep, guttural roar from halfway across the harbor. He hopped out of his chariot and sank into the deep water where the bottom of the stairs once were. He vanished below the crashing waves and a moment later I saw what looked like a blond squid struggling beneath the surface. The next moment Poseidon's head bobbed back into view and it looked like he was battling his way up the invisible underwater stone stairs.

The wife had nearly reached him just when he jumped from the chariot.

"*Honey, no!*" she hollered when his head came back into view.

From my vantage point among the ruins of some rich bastard's shattered yacht, I was the only one who could see all three of them. Poseidon missed completely Parka Man stepping right to the edge of the mall's back loading dock area. The scumbag in the sunglasses peeked through the weeds down the steep hill, and when he was sure Poseidon was doing the exact thing he'd hoped the god would do all along, he brought the trident down even with his shoulder and then swept it forward.

The water that had flooded the harbor responded like the first wave of a tsunami washing back out to sea. All the excess water fled in a matter of seconds, and in the instant just before the dolphin I was riding on and all the floating crap were swept out right along with the H2O, I caught a glimpse of Poseidon.

The god was suddenly high and dry standing on the steps leading up to the rear of the mall. He pulled a look on his face dumber than the one in his Olympus High class of 2000 B.C. yearbook as he glanced down at the monitor around his ankle. He managed to give one quick, worried look to his future widow, who was riding backwards on her dolphin and was in the process of being swept out to sea.

If you've never heard a god explode, it sounds a little like all four tires blowing out on the interstate at a hundred miles an hour, and it pretty much gives you the same uneasy feeling in the pit of your stomach that the whole world is about to end.

There was a distant explosion, a brilliant flash of light, and Poseidon was suddenly simply gone from the steps.

In the watery madness that had engulfed me in the harbor, I thought I caught sight of a shadow passing overhead, briefly blocking out the fire of the dying sun. Then the whole plight of dying gods became a whole hell of a lot less important to me as a billion gallons of rushing harbor water swept me, my dolphin, Mrs. Poseidon, and the broken debris of a couple of million's worth of future padded insurance claims out to sea.

12

My damn dolphin rode the waves like a trooper right up until he figured to hell with it and pitched me off. He took off without me for the safety of deeper waters. By then the worst of the tsunami was over and all I had to contend with was the equivalent of the city's floating landfill bashing me around the ocean's surface like the last pinball in the goddamn arcade.

I lost sight of the shore, mostly because of all the floating coolers and bobbing deck chairs that surrounded me an inch away from my nose. I could have been swept all the way back out to the middle of the ocean for all I knew, and with a dying sun turning the undersides of the orange clouds to molten lead in the swollen sky, I figured that while I was not literally up Shit Creek without a paddle I was bobbing around in the wine-dark sea equivalent which was, according to the National Oceanic and Atmospheric Administration, either the Shit Stream or El Shitto.

Fortunately my regular, prodigious intake of liquid refreshments stood me in good stead, and the fluid inside my body reached a cozy equilibrium with that on the outside which gave me time to splash around like a maniac

161

until I found a big enough floatable yacht cushion to keep my sorry ass from drowning.

"Mr. Banyon!"

I heard her before I saw her. I shoved aside a floating mini-fridge and found Miss Ravelli bobbing amongst the junk pile five feet away.

Once the fridge had floated aside I saw an area clear of debris wide open across the surface of the sea, like a field suddenly opening up in the middle of some woods. A very large, human-shaped mass was floating in the middle of the clearing, a gnarled knot of yellow hair spreading around the area under which there was, presumably, still a head.

"He's too heavy for me!" Miss Ravelli cried. "Help me!"

The dame didn't give me any choice. She grabbed the collar of my trench coat and swam like a launched missile for her bobbing husband.

He'd landed facedown in the water, and while he rose and fell with the waves I could see he wasn't breathing.

The pair of us struggled to turn him over, but the big goon wouldn't budge. She banged on his massive shoulder as if he was just kidding around and all he needed to wake up was a bit of hysterical terror and frustration from the little woman.

The monitor around his ankle was singed but still intact. The same was true for his ankle and foot. Yet the god wasn't breathing, and unless we managed to flip him over soon he most likely never would again.

The dame was losing it. She stopped whacking him in the shoulder and went back to trying desperately to roll the unmoving slab over onto his back.

Not that I liked the beach bum behemoth or anything; I still couldn't stand him. But it ticked me off that he'd come so close to getting the damned monitor off only to fall into Zeus' last-minute trap. It ticked me off even more that I'd taken the sea god and his wife on as clients and that once Zeus and co. were settled in at Poseidon's old address, the first thing the #1 god would probably do is make good on his threat to send one of Vulcan's thunderbolts straight through the grimy front window of Banjo Invest.

And when I thought of thunderbolts, I thought of Vulcan, and when I thought of that naked bastard I was suddenly shoving my fedora into Miss Ravelli's hands.

"Keep that dry, sister," I commanded.

I ducked below the waves, pawing around inside the pockets of my trench coat as I shoved myself around until I was underneath the sea god.

There wasn't even a single ray of weak, late-day sunlight underneath the massive nitwit's hulking carcass. I had to scrape away thick strands of hair until I cleared a path to his mouth. Once I'd excavated the big palooka's main head-hole, I slapped the item I'd fished from my pocket over his mouth and nose.

The metal ring from the bottom of the fish bowl on Vulcan's counter back on Olympus had jolted the water out of the way to create an oxygen tunnel. I didn't know if it'd work aimed down at the bottom of the ocean or if it'd be enough to revive the god.

The answer to my first question came immediately when I felt the warmth of open air suddenly brush across my arm beneath the surface of the murky sea. I pushed my face into the area below the open mouth of the bronze ring and it was suddenly like being back onshore. I took a deep breath of fresh oxygen, then rolled onto my back and gave Poseidon the biggest kick to the chest with both heels that I could manage.

The body only bobbed a little, and my underwater ballet act pretty much succeeded only in launching me deeper underwater. I Esther Williamsed my way back up and slapped the metal ring that I still clutched in my hand back over Poseidon's mouth.

The kick to the chest must have done the trick, because all at once the previously lifeless bulk floating above me was suddenly a thrashing bulk trying to drown the hell out of me.

I grabbed hold of Poseidon's shirt front and when the big idiot rolled over onto his back, I rode right along with him and back up into the air.

Poseidon was furious and disoriented, and I was just lucky he didn't see me first in that state or I'd have wound up a bloody mass of fish bait in a cheap suit. Instead he saw his wife, who flashed him a look of such great relief that his entire body relaxed. The tension went from his shoulders, the light went from his eyes, and he passed out cold.

Miss Ravelli paddled around and grabbed him around the neck, keeping the lunkhead lug from going under again.

"We have to get him to a doctor," she insisted.

I looked around at the crates and barrels that were bobbing around us, but failing to spot the emergency room entrance to a convenient floating Presbyterian hospital, I bobbed back around to face her.

"You know," I pointed out, "dames think it's their

birthright to have the toilet seat down at all times, like that is the one and only position nature intended. I never once in my life heard a guy complain because he had to lift the seat. We just shut up and do it."

She spit out a mouthful of water and frowned. "Are you telling me I should man up and drown?"

It was hard to shrug in the middle of the ocean, but somehow I managed. "I was actually telling you to shut up and drown, but if that's your takeaway, lady, swell."

Turns out she didn't have to do either. I suddenly felt something hard whack me in the back of the head, and unlike all the other hard crap that had been hitting me in the back of the head the previous ten minutes, this thing didn't float away.

I'd drifted up against a rock, and an instant after I'd felt the black basalt against my back, the soles of my shoes found the soft, welcome floor of a sandy shore. I grabbed onto the rock, shoved aside the flotsam that had followed us inland, pulled myself up, and discovered that I was staring into the grilles on a row of a bunch of parked cars. Beyond the cars I saw a parking lot, a little brick building, and high above it all the ominous optimism of a Burger King sign.

"Come on, let's hurry up and pull him down the shore," I quickly ordered Miss Ravelli, who'd just figured out the backwash from the harbor hadn't carried us out into the middle of the ocean after all. There were car engines and headlights and the nearby racket of people yapping away about enviably boring lives that didn't involve getting almost killed multiple times in a catastrophically interesting two day span.

"We can prop him up against the rocks right here and

call for help," she insisted.

"No, absolutely not here. By international fast food joint law, whatever washes up, down or otherwise makes it in or adjacent to a fast food parking lot via flood, backed-up storm drain or church fundraising car wash can be netted, breaded and deep fried. That goes double for horse-happy hamburger stands. This way."

I'd spotted a pay phone at a little park next-door. I made sure we kept below the rocks at the edge of the lot lest some fry jockey with a net and manager ambitions spot us.

I'd already seen Poseidon blow up once that day, and this time I was at ground zero. He might survive another blast, but the wife and I were Whopper meat if that bracelet around his ankle made it onto shore again. We were careful to keep the beeping ankle monitor submerged as the two of us went to work hauling the barely breathing god of the sea through the shallow water down the shoreline.

13

Night settled soft and dark across the grubby city streets, like the weatherproof custom car cover a panicked slob who's gone middle-aged nuts tosses over his midlife crisis Ferrari out in the driveway to protect it from evil until dawn. Except in the city the worst vices scuttle out at night and get trapped underneath the cloak of concealing darkness while high above the fetid streets, a dazzling array of bright, smiling stars give their twinkling blessing to the iniquitous pursuits of every scamming skunk, felonious lowlife and murderous bastard in town.

It was dark, the city lights had winked on, the storms that had raged out over the sea for days had finally died away, and I was still, regrettably, not plastered.

The only place in town equipped to take Poseidon was Holy Guacamole Mexican Memorial Hospital and Grill. They performed a lot of mermaid cosmetic surgery, so they had a water ambulance and a barge ward floating out behind the main hospital.

Poseidon was snoring in a peaceful coma in a reinforced bed, his barrel chest rising and falling underneath a crisp, white sheet.

The wife was a nervous wreck. She'd held it together

until we were almost to the hospital, but then lost it. She was more antsy than weepy, like a stool pigeon in the big house finally cornered by the rest of the flock he'd help send up the river.

I'd kept an eye on Poseidon while Miss Ravelli went to make a phone call. When she came back into the room her eyes were bloodshot from exhaustion.

"They're moving in right now," she said. "I talked to Zeus. He sends his regrets that his brother is going to die. I told him the doctors didn't say that at all, but Zeus was a lot more certain about it than them. He's going to finish him off, Mr. Banyon, I know it."

If she was looking for a comforting lie out of me, she'd picked the wrong P.I.

"You're right," I said. "The only thing you've got going for you right now is that Zeus and the rest of those SOBs are otherwise occupied. He and his thunderbolts will get around to it though, I guarantee it. What your old man needs is an equalizer."

She frowned. "You mean his trident. The water is calm now. It's all over the news. I saw it on the TV at the taco stand in the lobby. What makes you think this Makalooka, if that's even his name, didn't take the trident and leave
t   o   w   n   ?   "
"I'm thinking that this is personal for that bastard," I said. "He's not just some hired gun Zeus picked out of the back of *Soldier of Fortune*. If he knows Poseidon isn't dead, he'll find a way to finish him. I'm still on the clock until I track him down."

I started to leave the room, but the dame apparently didn't know the rules and grabbed my wrist, stepping all over my dramatic, tough-guy exit.

"Thank you, Mr. Banyon," she said. "If it wasn't for your quick thinking, I…well, I just wanted to make sure I thanked you, just in case…"

"I don't plan on being just-in-cased by some run-of-the-mill asshole in a parka," I assured her. "I'll handle him. I'm just not sure I can do anything about Zeus and the rest of those Olympus bastards squatting at your house. I can give you the number of an overweight shyster coincidentally named Shyster. Once he's finished with the distraction of bankrupting me, he can maybe try to sue their asses out of there."

"We'll be fine," she insisted. "I'm only worried about him right now." She nodded to her sleeping husband. "And anyway, until we figure something out we can always stay with the Zombie Cousteaus or Mr. and Mrs. Mollusk down the street."

A doctor in surgical scrubs and a sombrero came into the room and gave me the perfect cover I needed to slip out.

I heard him say, "Ah, Senorita Pescada!" real happy-like, like he knew the dame, and when I glanced back the door to the room was quickly closing.

Holy Guacamole Memorial was the same hospital where Doris was getting her tonsils ripped out, and I knew for sure that I'd get screeched at until my ears bled if she found out I'd been on the campus and hadn't stopped in. I checked my watch and saw that it was almost nine. Visiting hours were almost through, so I couldn't stay long. Besides, I didn't know how much work I'd get done that late, so I figured I'd swing in and pay my last respects to Doris' dearly departed tonsils. With any luck the surgeon slipped and clipped off the most venomous part of her tongue while he was in there.

I grabbed a couple of tulips from a flower bed in the garden on the path up to the side door and was shaking the dirt off the roots as I wandered up to the information desk.

"Doris Staurburton's room," I said to the fatso behind the counter.

I was still pretty wet from my swim in the sea, and even though I'd finally stopped dripping I could see the whale didn't approve of rumpled, damp private eyes.

She checked the computer but came up empty. "Spell it," she commanded, in that Gestapo-in-nylons tone common to hefty hospital dames.

I spelled the last name, and for good measure broke down "Doris" for her as well. She was scowling her tiny rosebud of twisted neon-red lipstick as she shook her head.

"No patient here by that name. No record of her being here in the past month. You sure you got the right hospital?"

She started spelling out the name of the hospital for me in that same slow-motion, short-bus way I'd spelled out "Doris" for her a minute before, which wasn't half as funny as when I'd done it. She hadn't gotten halfway through "guacamole" (and had gotten half the letters wrong, thanks to the local public school system) before I dropped the tulips with their muddy root balls on her counter and headed back out the automatic door.

There was a cab out front dumping off some elderly society broad. Holy Guacamole was on the train route, but I had a paying client for a change, and who am I to look a gift horse in the mouth? I waved the hack to stop and climbed in the back.

For a change, nobody tried to kill me on the way back to the office.

Vincetti's For the Halibut Fish Bazaar was closed for the night. Beats me if the cops were still holding him or if he'd just shut down until morning. If the old dago was smart he'd have stayed open twenty-four hours a day. The booming business he'd been experiencing the past couple of weeks as a result of Parka Man's screwing around with the sea was pretty much over. The customers who'd lined the sidewalk in front of his dump would soon be able to go back to the local supermarkets and actual reputable fish markets to pick up a catch of the day that hadn't been sealed in varnish.

I got out of my cab and was walking past the cartoon lobster in the window whose eyes old Vincetti frequently peeked out through, when I noticed some new additions to the pathetic scribblings on the particle boards on which the fishmonger advertised his rotting, shellacked merchandise.

Thrilled with his market's recent and inevitably temporary success, Vincetti was trying to expand his customer base even further by advertising "fish" in languages other than the usual English and Mussolini. Clearly he wanted to attract the passing eyes of the huddled masses yearning to puke free. Underneath the cartoon lobster I recognized invitations to explosive diarrhea written in French, German, Moon-Man, Esperanto, Serbian and Eskimo (not in my neighborhood, pal) and a dozen other languages. When I caught sight of one word in particular, I felt the final piece of a puzzle that had been nagging at the back of my head click into place.

"Vincetti, you greasy bastard, I owe you a free gondola ride," I said.

To repay the fishmonger for inadvertently clearing something up for me, I decided not to make my usual Thursday anonymous call to the health department that week.

I was so overwhelmed by my great generosity of spirit that when I entered my offices upstairs a minute later even the stink of fresh paint and varnish couldn't wipe the serene sense of smug from my kisser. I left my hat and coat on the rack that was still out in the outer room. I expected the worst as I shoved open the door to my office.

Mannix had finished his repairs. The floor was a lost cause. The hardwood was beautiful, shiny and new. The elf had tried to hide its perfection with a dirty rug he'd scrounged up from somewhere, but the gleaming edges peeked out near the walls. The rest of the joint looked as great as could be expected. He'd painted the walls in an ugly beige that was a reasonable facsimile of the old dirt-covered white I was so fond of.

My desk was weather-beaten perfection. If the kid ever tired of the pathetic life he'd made for himself as my office assistant, they'd be nuts at the Pole if they didn't welcome him back with open, stumpy arms.

There were a couple of large cloth sacks in front of my desk. I pulled open the drawstring on one and found the bag was stuffed with letters. I grabbed out a couple and saw the top one was addressed to "Poseidon, Fish God Bastard, Bottom of the Sea." The others were similarly addressed. The folks in the mailroom had managed to send out the letters like Miss Ravelli had asked before Zeus and his pals had muscled in.

I shoved the correspondence back into the bag and tugged the string shut.

As for the rest of my office, most of my usual crap was dumped back exactly where it belonged. The elf had outdone himself hauling the joint back into disreputable shape. I was lowering myself into my squeaky old chair when the outer door opened and I heard somebody enter Doris' office. A moment later, Mannix rolled a brand-new water cooler into my office.

"Oh, hello, Mr. Crag," the elf said. "I didn't know you were back."

"Yes, Mannix," I said. "I'm back because this is where you and I come to work. Doris, on the other hand, stops in only to make sure her curlers are still plugged in just in case she's ever in the neighborhood and finds herself in need of an emergency perm."

The elf didn't seem to know what to say. His guilty grapefruit-sized eyes darted to the four corners of the room. He suddenly remembered that he had a distraction sitting on the dollie he'd just lugged into the room, and he quickly hiked the new water cooler up and rolled it into the corner where the old one had exploded.

There was no sense torturing Mannix. I left him to his work setting the water cooler in the exact same spot, down to the millimeter, as the old one.

As Mannix worked, I pulled out my piece and shook the four remaining slugs out onto my blotter. Who knew what my encounter with Parka Man would bring, and I'd spent so much time in the drink the past two days that I wanted to make sure it was cleaned and ready to split open a zinc-smeared nose at a hundred paces.

The elf must have heard me grunt, because he stopped rocking the dollie out from under the cooler and glanced up at me examining my roscoe at my desk.

"Is something wrong, Mr. Crag?"

"There have been a few very rare moments in my life where everything hasn't been completely wrong, Mannix," I said. "This moment goes on the wall of fame as one of those unusually brief instances where more than one thing has gone right for me."

The elf seemed to want to tell me something, but he didn't want to break the mood. He opened and closed his mouth a few times, then gave up and grabbed onto the dollie. I didn't give him a chance to wheel it out of the office.

"Spill it, Mannix," I ordered.

His little shoulders slumped. "I tried to find out about Miss Ravelli like you asked," the elf said. "My friend at the North Pole wouldn't give me anything from her naughty or nice file. He said they didn't even have anything about her in any of their human records, which is impossible. I told him that lying is a naughty thing to do, but it didn't help. I'm sorry, Mr. Crag."

The elf seemed to want to feel bad about disappointing me, so he didn't know how to react when I flashed him an annoying, shit-eating grin.

"Savor the moment, Mannix," I suggested. "And when you're finished savoring the hell out of it, get me the phonebook."

I quickly cleaned my gat, scrounged up a couple replacement bullets that I found rolling around in the back of my desk drawer, and very carefully loaded all six slugs into my piece, which I holstered with a little less of my normal carelessness.

Mannix brought in the office phonebook, which looked like Doris had used it to mop up the Exxon Valdez of spilled fingernail polish. I tossed the book with the illegible, stuck-together pages in the trash.

"Find me one that hasn't been caught in the blast radius of one of Doris' Mary Kay bombs," I said. "Bust into Wasserbaum's office if you have to."

I knew the elf wouldn't do it. B & E was naughty, and he had a nasty nice streak. He hustled from the office on his mission and, lacking a phonebook, I reluctantly surrendered to one of the least exciting aspects of P.I. work: reading crackpot mail.

It's not like you don't sometimes hit pay dirt digging through old letters. When I was with the cops I worked a case where one of those giant talking eggs had a great fall off a wall. What the hell he was doing out there in the first place was a mystery. First theory was he'd cracked and committed suicide. That was until we went through his old mail we found hidden in the vegetable crisper of the fridge where he lived. Turns out he'd gotten a bunch of threatening notes in the previous month. We were able to lift a good hoof print from one, and thanks to that we managed to nail one of the King's horses. It all came out at the trial. The egg had poached the horse's wife, and their embryonic romance had ended when the cuckolded equine had shoved the ovum lothario out onto the wall and scrambled him up real good. In the end it was the horse who fried.

I wasn't looking forward to poring through this particular batch of mail since the Poseidons were celebrities. The really famous always attract a hell of a lot more mail from crazies, and that went double for gods.

The sheer volume of mail was daunting. I poked around in the bags a little and found that the stuff had at least been sorted so that the most recent mail was in one bag, the correspondence from six months to a year back was in another and so on.

I found at the top of the nearest bag the note Miss Ravelli had shown me on the back deck of The Seaweed Palace Bar.

The cut-and-paste job was still lousy, but it was the "your next" that caught my eye. The first time I'd seen it I assumed I was dealing with an illiterate. It's not like American high schools and colleges aren't dumping a surplus of those on us every spring. This time, however, I thought of Parka Man.

I'd heard him speak two of the times he attacked me. First time at the health bar it was "me want him" and then at O'Hale's it was "where Banyon." The continental U.S. didn't have the exclusive on crummy schools, and he certainly could have graduated with straight As in English from Honolulu High (rah-rah, Fighting Pineapples). On the other hand it was Jaublowski the certified moron who'd said Hawaiian back at the bar, and I'd taken a vacation from good sense and let it get locked in my stupid brain.

I did a little rooting around near the top of the bag and found a bundle of letters separate from the rest and bound up with a rubber band.

Miss Ravelli had her husband's Water World post office keep the real threatening mail separate. Skipping through the dates I saw that the bundle was just the stuff that had started in the past couple of weeks. Zeus had expected Poseidon to blow up long before then, so this was the desperate mail that was meant as bait. Scare the wife, work the idiot husband into a rage, trick him up on shore. I had to admit, it worked like a charm.

The postmarks were all from some place called Gagoonda. I'd never heard of the dump, and I had to pull out an atlas to look it up. Turned out it was an island out in the middle of the Pacific, not only nowhere near Hawaii, it was nowhere near anything.

The postmark was two curved palm trees framing the face of a scowling native. That face looked awfully familiar, so I took out a black pen and drew a fringe of a parka around the head and colored in a pair of dark glasses. Sure enough, Gagoonda's postmark was a picture of the bastard who kept trying to murder me.

I checked through the Gagoonda mail and found it was all pretty much the same: "me kill you," "you die soon," "I homicide you up real good."

I had all the letters spread out on my desk in front of me when Mannix returned fifteen minutes later with a phonebook.

"Be careful with it, Mr. Crag," the elf said as he handed it over with the reverence reserved for Gutenberg Bibles. "Mr. Lou from the diner down the street is renting it to me for ten dollars an hour."

The kind spirits in this town make my soul weep with love for my fellow man.

Mannix examined the envelopes on my desk as I flipped the book open to local motels. Parka Man was from out of town, and the likeliest joints for him to rent a room were near the shore. I'd start with the beachfront flophouses and work my way inland.

"Gagoonda?" Mannix asked as I dialed the number to 1-Star Bedbug Economy Roomette Suites. The elf scrunched up his nose like he recognized the name.

He didn't give me a chance to tell him to buzz off before he turned and hustled out of my office. I heard him log onto the Internet from the computer Doris used to keep track of her goddamn Facebook farm.

It took five phone calls to five fleabag motels, the last one actually being The Fleabag Motel, which was a small chain within the Hilton Hotels Corporation empire. Forget everything you've seen on TV about having to bribe or fast-talk minimum wage desk clerks, especially the poor slobs on the night shift. They either aren't bright enough to recognize a con, or they plain don't give two shits. I didn't need a lot of fancy scamming to find out that Parka Man was registered at the Fleabag under the name Dr. Winston Q. Churchill McSecret, and that he'd left ten minutes before.

"He carrying a trident with him?" I asked.

"You kiddin' me? Guy got that thing on him at all times. Cleaning broad tried to move it once and she mysteriously drowned when the room's waterbed exploded and pinned her to the wall. We don't clean that room no more. They's coconut husks and banana peels lying all over the goddamn place. It stinks like one of them there tropical paradises they got over in that what-you-call place. Oceania, and like that, you know?"

"You have any idea where he went?" I asked. "This expensive ice cream cake he ordered is melting like a bastard." (Luckily, I didn't exactly have to haul out my A-level con artist shell game with that dope.)

"How the hell should I know?" the desk clerk said.

"He did say on the way out that he was in the mood for his native cuisine, you know? Could be anywhere."

Could be. Wasn't. I figured I had a pretty good idea where he'd gone.

I thanked the desk clerk and hung up. I hustled out to the outer office and grabbed my hat and coat from the rack. Mannix looked up excitedly as I was shrugging on my trench coat.

"Gagoonda," the elf said. "I thought I remembered that name. It was on TV last May during Tsunami Week on NBC. It was one of the first islands that got swamped. The ratings were very high for that episode, Mr. Crag. There were only fifty natives living on Gagoonda, but after sweeps there was only one left."

He spun the computer screen around and there was Parka Man, sans parka.

The poor bastard looked pretty miserable standing on a beach by himself. Turns out the postmark got high marks for accuracy. All that was left of Gagoonda after the flood-waters more-or-less receded was one waterlogged SOB and two sagging palm trees. There were remnants of crushed grass huts, raw sewage and a couple of giant cast iron missionary stewpots you can pick up at Macy's floating around the white sandy shore.

Mannix had pulled up an AP story about the devastation. I didn't read the rest of the article since the headline and caption under the photo told me all I needed to know.

LAST SURVIVING GAGOONDAN BLAMES POSEIDON

"NOT MY FAULT," CLAIMS GOD OF SEA: "TEC-TONIC PLATES, ZEUS"

The photo's caption read, "New Gagoondan President-by-default Makalooka watches island nation's only toilet seat float by, swears vengeance."

So the poor bum was already wound up, all he needed was a push in the right direction from stage manager Zeus.

"Nice work, Mannix," I said. "You can bring the phonebook back. Tell Lou if he doesn't refund five bucks for the half hour we didn't use it, I'm going to tell everyone I know that he gets all his fresh fish at Vincetti's. He'll be out of business in a week."

"Yes, sir, Mr. Crag. Where are you going this late?"

"To a restaurant even worse than Lou's that I already know is going out of business in a week."

14

If the fact that Elmhurst Ends wasn't becoming one of the worst neighborhoods in town thanks to all the trolls, a lousy name like A Tiny Taste of Zimbabwe would have eventually put out of business the dirty little restaurant on the corner of William Howard Taft Boulevard and the unnamed dead end that led to the east end of Anus Park.

I probably wouldn't have even remembered it was there if not for the fact that Doc Minto had just mentioned the restaurant back at O'Hale's the day before while the old M.E. was pawing around inside that zombie corpse. The dump was within walking distance of both the bay where Parka Man had been spending his days tormenting the ocean and the Fleabag Motel where he'd been spending his nights squeezing burrowing bedbug larvae out of his subcutaneous layer of skin.

I'd already guessed Gagoondan President Makalooka wasn't hankering for a Little Caesar's two-topping special. Mannix's research just confirmed it.

Most of the city's cannibal eateries were put out of business when Washington made it illegal to donate a loved one's body to lunch back during the Sixties. I'd read in the *Gazette* a few years back that the Zimbabwean joint had gotten a major influx of dough from a deposed African finance minister who'd paid the owner ten percent for allowing him to park a couple million in his bank account. If it wasn't for that terrific stroke of luck from a random email, A Tiny Taste wouldn't have lasted as long as it had.

The lobby was lined with zebra and Jehovah's Witnesses heads. The bored coat check girl offered to take my spear and ceremonial witch doctor mask, which she didn't notice I'd left in my grass hut back in the veldt. I don't even think the dame looked at me once. She just sighed this miserable, prolonged exhale and continued picking the legs off the luckless tarantula on her counter that had wandered in from the lunch menu.

The main dining room was done up with murals of sweeping African vistas, plastic booths and track lighting. Communal tables were arranged around six giant cast-iron cooking pots. It was like Benihana where the chef prepares your stir fry right in front of your nose, except at A Tiny Taste of Zimbabwe there was no rice and the teriyaki was imported missionary in a white wine sauce with orange slices and parsley.

The restaurant had never even caught on even with college hipsters, which was fine by me. I got stuck on a bus with two of those privileged bums a couple years back, and they spent the whole ride across town loudly complaining about how the service was lousy and how stringy the undercooked Catholics were.

I found Parka Man sitting alone and perusing the menu at the only occupied table in the whole dining room. His sunglasses were off and sitting at his elbow on the corner of the table. The Zimbabwean owner kept the restaurant steamy, so it was likely that for the first time since coming to the good old U.S. of A. the Gagoondan skunk was as warm as he was back home. He'd pulled down his hood and unzipped his parka halfway. He wore a lobster bib with a cartoon priest on a plate drawn on it and a big smile on his face. The grin vanished when he happened to glance up and saw me marching straight at him across the dining room floor.

The son of a bitch was fast, I'd give him that. I hadn't even seen the trident leaning against the table. He had it up and whipped around in my direction before I'd even made it halfway across the floor.

Every missionary-sized iron pot in the restaurant began to hum like a half-dozen dinner gongs, and started rattling frantically on their bases like six lunch specials had awakened simultaneously and were trying to escape back to the rectory.

The water in the pots exploded up like it had been shot from six fire hoses. Water glasses on a few of the tables shattered and their contents fired up as well, joining the swirling storm of water that was spinning in place around the ceiling like a flushed toilet that refused to go down.

I felt a rumble under my feet, and I could hear groaning pipes bursting one after another.

Horns started honking like mad outside and I knew the water main had ruptured. Same deal with the panicked shouts from the kitchen. I heard more groaning metal from behind the silver doors and I knew from the crashes that sinks were busting off walls.

A second later and the chef and wait staff came running for all they were worth through the swinging kitchen doors. A spray of water chased them through both the in and out doors as they ran screaming for the emergency exit near the restaurant's stuffed Episcopalian mascot. The coat check girl abandoned her two-legged spider and stumbled like mad for the main door, only to be thrown back inside by the wall of water that had just burst in from the street.

The problem for Parka Man this time was that he didn't seem to understand that I was finally wise to his game. This time he didn't have an ocean of water, the element of surprise or exploding porcelain fixtures to back him up. This time it was just me and him, and as much water as he could throw at me in that one room before I reached him.

He reeled back, and with a demented look sent all the water he'd collected up at the ceiling streaming right for me. Unlucky for him I was close enough that all I had to do was snatch up a chair and keeping on barreling right at him.

The water from the street and kitchen couldn't get to me fast enough. All I had to contend with was the stuff from the ceiling, and even though it knocked me back for a second when it hammered the underside of the chair, I just kept right on going.

The water broke around the chair. My arms strained at the pressure, but I knew it wouldn't last because by then I'd reached old Parka Boy. When I got to him, I didn't stop. The seat slammed the bastard at a full sprint and he went up and over, tumbling off his chair. I saw bare feet and bits of grass skirt flying up in the air, and I saw the trident go flipping from his hand and skittering underneath the next table.

Without the bastard to direct it, every drop of airborne

water suddenly lost interest in playing drown the P.I. The water stopped dead, hovered in the air for a second, then dropped like a two-second monsoon to the restaurant's threadbare carpet with the ketchup stains on the African safari motif.

"No!" Parka Man shouted as he scrambled to his feet. "You not alive! Banyon dead! Banyon dead!"

He was clearly begging for a demonstration that his assumption was incorrect, and after all the times he'd tried to kill me in the past two days I was in an instructive mood. I grabbed him by the lobster bib and played the joker a symphony of chin music, sending a couple of his bloody ivories scattering to the concert hall floor.

The eyes rolled back, the life went from the bow legs, and Makalooka, president of Gagoonda, went down for the count on the carpet in an inch-deep puddle over the worn-out trunk of a sickly-looking hand-stitched elephant.

Water rolled in lazily from the kitchen. I heard cars honking and people yelling outside, but without Parka Man to direct it, the water from the busted pipes out in the street no longer rushed through the front door.

A few of the Tiny Taste staff peeked in from the front hall. I waved them in and got one of the kitchen help to give me his apron, which I used to tie up Makalooka.

"Call the cops," I ordered. "Ask for Detective Dan Jenkins. I can't think of anyone else on the force who deserves to clean up a mess this big."

I filched a napkin from Makalooka's table, shook it out and used it to pull the trident out from where it had slid, careful to keep the cloth wrapped around one of the tines. There'd be prints on the thing if the cops decided to come looking for it, and I sure as hell didn't want any of them to be mine.

I saw the bastard's sunglasses lying on the floor and figured I could use them later on. I scooped them up, too, and stuffed them in the breast pocket of my suit jacket.

I left Parka Man sopping wet and tied up on the floor in his gnarled grass skirt that looked like a maniac's front yard after a downpour.

When I headed to the side exit, half the staff of A Tiny Taste of Zimbabwe were poking him with a spatula while in the flooding kitchen the chef was cutting a huge pat of butter into the biggest frying pan I'd ever seen. I was deeply disappointed when I slapped open the door and heard the approach of distant police cruisers.

"No wonder you're going out of business," I muttered. "You have no concept of American fast food. If you'd deep fried instead of grilled, he'd be done by now."

They were hoisting Makalooka into the air and spiriting him into the kitchen as I slipped out the door with Poseidon's trident clutched tight in my hand and, for the first time in days, a song in my blissful bastard heart.

15

When I returned to the barge ward floating out behind Holy Guacamole Mexican Memorial Hospital and Grill, I found a whole herd of middle-aged heifers in gigantic white skirts and starched white hats giggling around the nurses' station.

All the fatso nurses were in swooning overdrive. I knew it was rotten news when I saw they were so busy gabbing that they'd left their takeout ice cream order to melt in the paper bag on the counter.

"He's so handsome."

"Oh, yes. I can see why *People* named him the sexiest god of the year in 1500 B.C."

One of them who looked like a bison in white panty-hose waved an autograph over her head, announced it was from Zeus and said that he'd promised to take her in his Lamborghini Chariot ZG001 to gather clouds in Asia Minor on Saturday. The rest of the round-up mooed over their gargantuan colleague's great luck. They'd been so effectively distracted that not one of them was paying attention to the room down the hall.

I heard the sound of a struggle even before I reached the door. When I ran into the room I found Zeus with a pillow in his hands going *Cuckoo's Nest* Indian Chief on Poseidon's face. The sea god was flailing around in the bed trying to fight his brother off.

Miss Ravelli was pounding her fists on Zeus' back trying to get him to drop the pillow. The dame was bawling her eyes out and screaming for help, but the twenty head of nurse down the hall weren't budging from their grazing station.

When I burst into the room, the wife looked up all pleading-like, but when I took out my gat she shook her head that it wouldn't be enough.

"Out of the way, sweetheart," I ordered.

She obligingly left the bedside, giving me a clean shot at Zeus. At the sound of my voice, the hulking king of the gods in his lounge lizard Seventies outfit glanced over his beefy shoulder. The lower half of his salon tanned face pulled down in a frown.

"I warned you, Banyon," Zeus said, looking like a pissed-off seven-foot Bee Gee in Mr. T chains. "I told you not to take this case. You're next."

He kept both hands pressed firmly into the pillow over Poseidon's mug. The fight was draining from the sea god's steroid-pumped arms.

"Step away from the fish stick," I ordered. "You only get one warning."

Zeus laughed. "You think some mortal pea shooter is a match for an Olympian?" he mocked. "The heavens obey my commands, Banyon. The goddamn *heavens*."

"I don't order around the stars," I admitted, "but I do my best with my little corner of this crummy town. You were warned."

Three shots. I was real careful to count. A couple of

warm kisses from Misters Smith and Wesson to the shoulder and Zeus dropped the pillow and wheeled on me.

There was a little blood through his green nylon polo shirt, but not anything like the human level plasma you get from three point-blank blasts. I figured he was already healing, and my guess was confirmed when I heard a sound like three dropped pebbles and I saw my slugs fall to the floor and roll away behind him.

The king god shook off what amounted to a trio of bug bites and approached me with fresh rage. He held out his hand like I'd seen him do back on Olympus, and the first flicker from the ball of glowing fire formed the size of a marble in his palm.

"When I'm finished with you, there won't even be so much as one cinder left for the janitor to sweep up," Zeus growled.

"Admittedly, your plan is probably neater than mine," I said, nodding. "My plan, on the other hand, has the benefit of the element of surprise."

"Plan?" he scoffed. "What plan? Why are you putting on those sunglasses?"

I'm better at show and tell than twenty questions.

This time when I pulled the trigger there was a flash of light like something from the birth of the universe. The blast threw me back against the sink in the corner of the room. A pile of tongue depressors flew everywhere and a cardboard box of rubber gloves smacked me on the head on its way to the floor.

I knew enough to close my eyes behind Parka Man's shades, but the light still permeated my eyelids. I blinked away stars as I struggled to my feet.

The room was coming back into focus. Zeus lay

stunned on the floor. His head had made a V-shaped dent in the baseboard heat. The king of the gods looked a hell of a lot smaller than he did before. He was no longer the towering six-foot-plus SOB who'd strode around his temple on Olympus, threatened me, swiped his brother's undersea kingdom or made time with every babe in every Cretan schoolyard and barnyard. One thunderbolt to the chest looked like it had done a mortal number on him. But being the professional that I am, I figured I'd make sure.

"Here," I said, reaching under my coat. "Finish it, will you? I don't feel like looking over my shoulder for incoming thunderbolts the rest of my life." Poseidon was coming around on the bed, and when I tossed the god his trident and he snatched it from the air the resultant surge of energy that coursed through the room made the hairs on the back of my neck stand on end.

Miss Ravelli was stumbling to her feet over by the bathroom door. She didn't seem to know what to make of what had just happened. She saw her husband newly invigorated in his bed, she saw what looked like the mortal version of Zeus struggling to his feet over by the baseboard heater, and she saw me coming over and grabbing her by the arm.

It turned out Parka Man was like a kindergarten kid who'd gotten hold of a box of paints and a brush. Put the trident in the hands of the master, and you had Michelangelo.

Poseidon raised the trident. The ship in which we were floating groaned.

He whipped it down.

The bulkhead burst apart and a sliver of water that

grew into a fat serpent-like stream shot into the room. The coil of water wrapped around Zeus' neck like the end of a whip, and the last thing I saw as I hustled the dame out into the hallway was Zeus flying around the room banging off every wall.

The nurse herd pounded past us down the hall on massive hoofs. The stampede stopped outside Poseidon's door and the dames in white were justifiably horrified at the brutal beating that was going on inside. The most gigantic of the mammoths lumbered back to the desk to place a frantic, fat call to security.

"How—" was all Miss Ravelli managed to ask.

I still held my gat in my hand. I gave a real casual shrug.

"I gave Vulcan a bullet to copy," I said as I holstered my piece. "I didn't realize until after I blew away your husband's sea monster ex-girlfriend back at your place that he'd even given me that one thunderbolt. I sure as hell had no idea until I got back to my office and cleaned my roscoe that he'd kept the original and made me two. Guy was pretty bored. Guess he was showing off. Don't worry, it'll all be on your itemized bill. Hey, sounds like the party is wrapping up. You better get back, Senorita Pescada."

I gave the dame a big wink and watched her face fall as I turned away.

Down the hallway, the fat nurses were appalled, some doctors in sombreros with bandoliers wrapped in X-shapes over the chests of their scrubs were running in from the siesta ward to see what was going on, and the metal walls of the old converted scow were denting out into the hall in suspiciously Zeus-shaped lumps.

I made it up topside in time to hear the metal side of the boat ward tear open as if it had been ripped apart by the can opener on a giant Swiss army knife. I saw the speck that was the mortal remains of Zeus sail far out over the sea and disappear into the night beyond the warm glow of the peaceful harbor lights.

I doubt I could've heard the splash when it came even if I wasn't whistling a jaunty-assed tune as I marched across the gangplank to the shore and ultimately, with luck, to the end of several days of god-induced goddamn sobriety.

16

The only part of the job I generally don't hate is writing up a client's bill, mostly because unlike every other part of the work I usually don't nearly get killed doing it.

The Poseidons had paid a flat fee upfront and there wasn't a lot of miscellaneous crap to add up. I billed them for the bullets I'd bought from Vulcan along with the imported Greek booze. (That false sense of security I lulled the naked blacksmith god into by making him think I was just another Olympus tourist was a stroke of P.I. genius.) A little cab fare here, some dry cleaning there, the cost of the new water cooler Mannix hadn't told me he put on the credit card I didn't know I had. All in all, only a couple hundred bucks in expenses. A bargain at twice the price.

The week after I'd saved the day like the hero bastard that I am, I had their bill on my desk in the to-be-mailed basket. I'd also finally tracked down Doris.

For the first dozen times I called her house, that old bat mother of hers stonewalled and insisted that Doris was in the hospital recovering from tonsil surgery. I finally got the nasty biddy to put Doris on the phone by cleverly threatening to come over and burn down her house if she didn't. When Doris came on the line she tried to make her voice sound rasping, but she was as crummy an actress as she was a secretary.

"You are not, Doris, recovering from surgery. You weren't in the hospital you said you were going to be in — don't interrupt, Doris — I checked, and you weren't in any hospital in town. Since you're home and not on some godforsaken kitsch vacation with that hag who spawned you—" (A horrified gasp and I knew the hag herself was listening in on the extension.) "—I assume your absence is hair-, nail- or makeup-related."

She snarled, she exhaled, and finally she spit, "I got my hair done, Crag Banyon, what's it to you?"

"I care, Doris, because I should have a smiling face in my outer office to greet clients. Until I find one that eases up on the clown makeup I'm stuck with yours, but that arrangement only works if you're actually popping that wad of gum out at your desk."

"You're a rat," Doris insisted. "I'm entitled to some of them personal days like other secretaries get. I just been spoilin' you is all. You ain't got no clue that good secretaries are hard to find."

"That is true," I conceded, "which is why I never set my sights that high. Lousy secretaries are, on the other hand, a dime a dozen. They're flunking out at Miss Beauregard's School of Cosmetology across the street every day. I could holler out the window right now and get three applicants. Even a dame too dumb to bleach hair can answer a phone. My cup runneth over. So what's it going to be? You still work here?"

"You're a bastard, Crag Banyon."

"See you bright and early tomorrow morning," I replied.

As I hung up the phone I could hear both Doris and her old bag mother screeching up a storm.

Mannix was standing at the open door to my office and had heard the whole exchange. "Will Miss Doris be coming to work tomorrow?" the elf asked.

"Hope springs eternal," I said, "but I wouldn't bet the ranch."

"I'm glad, Mr. Crag," Mannix nodded. "Gambling is naughty."

"The way I do it counts as charity. Speaking of which, here. Outgoing mail."

I held the Poseidon bill out to him. I probably saved the little guy's life, since the moment he stepped from the door there was a flash of light and a crack of thunder. All the loose paperwork and dust swirled around my office like somebody had set a tornado loose on the third floor, and I knew what to expect once the squall settled.

There stood Mercury, messenger of the displaced Olympian gods. I hadn't expected he'd be accompanied by Mr. and Mrs. Poseidon.

Poseidon was back to full strength. The sea god's broad shoulders filled the doorframe, and one mighty hand gripped Mercury by the back of the neck. The wife stood before the sea god, beside the messenger god, and tried not to look guilty.

"Speak of the devil," I said. "You saved me a stamp. Mannix?"

The elf plucked the bill from my hand and delivered it to Mrs. Poseidon. After he'd handed it off, he kept on going past Poseidon's massive thigh and into the outer office where he started battering nervously away at the Smith Corona.

"This guy gave you a problem last week," Poseidon announced. He rattled Mercury around like a four-limbed maraca. "He's here to make amends."

I'd told the wife about the threatened lawsuit from Schmecky Shyster after we'd first brought the comatose sea god to Holy Guacamole.

"No need," I said. "After I left you at the hospital last week, I met Mitchell Fraud of the illustrious Shyster, Pilfer and Fraud law firm chasing an ambulance into the Holy Guacamole parking lot. He's younger and hungrier than the other senior partners and has the best running shoes. After he finished passing out business cards to everyone in the emergency room, I hired him to sue partner Schmecky Shyster for inflicting emotional distress on me by threatening to sue me for inflicting emotional distress on him. It put the whole law firm into a jurisprudent chicken-and-the-egg causality loop, the upshot of which is that nobody is suing anybody or the universe might explode."

"Oh," Poseidon said. He shook a very miserable-looking Mercury for the sheer hell of it. "You're still paying for that window."

The sea god bounced the messenger god from my office. The wife lingered.

"I wanted to thank you for everything you did, Mr. Banyon," she said.

I waved a magnanimous hand. "Prompt payment for services rendered is all the thanks I require."

Something was eating the dame. I figured I knew what. Once the husband was gone, she shut the door on my outer office.

"What you said at the hospital…" she began.

"You're really a mermaid," I said. (Why beat around

the bush? Besides, I had a barstool that was probably so panicked that it hadn't seen me in days that it was filing a missing person report on me.) "That's why no family was there to cheer you on at the Olympics and why you have no real life history before then, and no human naughty or nice record at the North Pole. I figure you appropriated somebody else's ID, probably a kid who died at birth whose family members have all died since then. I knew something was fishy about you, I just didn't know what. Poseidon said back in your kitchen that you were visiting your sister when Makalooka stole the trident, and I filed that one away in the curious bullshit category since you have no family, at least according to every source we here at Banjo Invest were able to track down. That doctor calling you Senorita Pescada was the last clue I needed. He knew you. Probably operated on you, since they do mermaido-plasties at Holy Guacamole. Pescada is Spanish for fish, which I'd forgotten but was reminded of thanks to old Vincetti the rancid fishmonger downstairs. The garbage you're always drinking is the equivalent of hormones for sex-changed humans. I looked it up. It keeps you from sprouting scales on those pretty gams of yours. Simple."

"You're a clever man, Mr. Banyon."

"Not too bright," I said. "I should have known when you were the only one that Russian shark didn't eat at the Bongo Congo games. Everybody knows sharks hate mer-maids. They give them the flaming fish shits. That's also why those two shark-men turned tail and ran down at your undersea palace."

The dame looked absolutely miserable that her secret had been uncovered.

"All my records, my endorsements, my silver medal,

my good work for the Swimmer's Ear Foundation…it will all be undone when this gets out."

She was deeply distraught, clearly imagining her entire world was over. I got up from behind my desk and went over, taking her by the arm and patting her hand.

"Lucky for you, then, that I, like every other sensible individual in the entire human race, don't give a steaming shit on a trampoline about Olympic swimming."

I'm the king of goddamn compassion.

I led her from the office, past typing Mannix and out into the hallway, managing to snag my hat and coat along the way.

"My husband—" she began, sniffling.

"Doesn't know? Does know? Who cares, doll? It's Olympic swimming."

She was composed when we picked up her husband on the second floor.

Poseidon got on the elevator alone. The cable groaned as the doors closed.

"Mercury is working off his debt," he announced to his wife. If he noticed by her puffy eyes that she'd nearly been blubbing a moment ago, he didn't show it. "The rest of them are back on Olympus, at least for now. With Zeus gone, the Greeks are overrunning the place. There won't be one piece of marble standing on another by the end of the week. Serves all them right. Let them all go to Hades. He's got the room."

"Did the cops want your trident to lift prints?"

"Some cop named Jenkins called. I told him if he wanted it, I'd be happy to shove it through his head. He said he probably didn't need it after all."

"Too bad," I said. "I would've bought a front row ticket.

Anyway, assuming Parka Boy isn't negotiating his way
through the digestive systems of several Tiny Taste of
Zimbabwe employees, they've got enough of a case against
that Gagoondan bastard even without the trident. They've
got pictures of him at the scene at the shore, he killed some
hotel maid plus a couple dozen taffy shop customers and
employees, and cost millions in property damage. With or
without your trident as evidence, the little grass skirt-
wearing SOB will be going away for a long time."

We parted on the sidewalk out front. Poseidon gave
me a hearty smack on the shoulder that nearly dislodged
my eyeballs and the little woman nodded silent thanks.
The pair of them left arm-in-arm, god of the sea and his
trans-species ex-mermaid wife. Hey, whatever gets somebody through the day. I don't judge.

I was already in a buoyant mood as I struck off alone
down the street, and I got a hell of a lot more upbeat when
Vincetti jumped desperately out the front door of the For
the Halibut Fish Bazaar as I walked by. The old fishmonger
had mistaken me for a customer, a species to which he'd
mistakenly grown accustomed and which had abandoned
him days before. When he saw it was me, the peddler of
antediluvian fish turned around and beat a hasty retreat
back inside his reeking establishment.

The world was my oyster and, happily, since I hadn't
bought this particular shellfish at Vincetti's it wasn't loaded
down with bacteria that would turn my organs to mashed
potatoes and cause my bowels to detonate like a
Claymore.

When I reached O'Hale's, I was careful not to be too
goddamn ebullient as I pushed open the door and stepped
into the gloom.

"Heya, Jinx, what'll you have?" asked a suspiciously cheerful voice that sounded like Jaublowski's and came from a head that looked like Jaublowski's but could not possibly have belonged to Ed Jaublowski.

I'd dodged O'Hale's for days since I figured the barkeep would be holding a grudge for all the damage Parka Man had done. Jaublowski's suspiciously happy greeting had the effect of a fire extinguisher on the candle that was my good mood.

There were a few fresh bottles on a shelf behind the bar to replace the dozens of watered-down booze bottles Parka Man had blown up. Jaublowski was pouring me a drink before I'd even parked myself on my regular stool.

The door to the men's room was propped open and I could see a pile of deceased porcelain stacked up in the middle of the still-soggy floor. At least the pipes were still off so the water was not gushing again, and I saw that somebody had made a half-assed effort to mop up the water that had flooded out into the bar. The damp mop was still leaning up against the wall, where I assumed it would still be standing when the meteor that was scheduled to hit the city finally struck in nine years.

"I see you're letting bygones be bygones," I said. I held the glass up to one of the dim lights behind the bar. "Arsenic or strychnine?"

"I ain't got no reason to hold no grudge, Jinx," Jaublowski insisted. "I got federal flood disaster relief. All us flooded businesses all over town is getting checks. Everybody with water damage gets something. Pennies from heaven, Jinx. Goddamn free money. Didn't you put in for none?"

"Regrettably, I took responsibility and fixed my damage

myself," I said.

"You's always been a sap, Jinx. It ain't costing nobody nothing. Government mailed me a check worth way more than that dump-of-a-bathroom was ever worth. Maybe I'll put in a trough. It'd be cheaper and I can pocket the difference."

"I don't suppose I can persuade you to invest some of that largess in soap and paper towels?"

It was as if any talk of cleanliness didn't even register with Jaublowski.

"That's not all we's gettin' outta this one, Jinx. You know that law firm what's in your building? Shyster, Pilfer and Fraud?"

"I am passingly familiar with the firm."

"Yeah, well, Marvin Pilfer's organizing a huge lawsuit against that bastard what flooded all the joints around town. He's promising us millions, Jinx. *Millions.*"

"They are undeniably talented ambulance chasers, Ed, witnessed firsthand by yours truly, but I think even they're going to have a hard time with that one seeing as how the slob is likely dead and his country is a dead broke island with no other inhabitants."

Jaublowski twisted one side of his mouth practically up into his ear in a pitying scowl. "Geez, Jinx, ain't you seen a paper?"

He reached below the bar and tossed a two-day old copy of the *Gazette* down in front of me. It was a front-page story. The U.S. had taken out a third mortgage on everything West of the Rockies, and borrowed a couple more billion from China, turned it over as foreign aid to Gagoonda and stuck the taxpayers with the tab.

There was a picture on the front page of the *Gazette*.

Makalooka was clearly in one hell of a lot less trouble with the local cops than I thought. In the photo, he was standing back on his sorry excuse for a tropical beach flanked by that selfsame pair of sagging palm trees as before.

Most of the garbage that had been floating around the remains of Gagoonda in the picture Mannix had found in last year's paper had washed up on the beach. The tiny little shore of the miserable excuse for an island was so covered with crap it looked like somebody had dumped the contents of Doris' desk drawers into a cat box.

Makalooka's parka was gone and his hands and knees were burned and partially bandaged, presumably saved from sautéing by the cops who'd invaded A Tiny Taste of Zimbabwe. The asshole secretary of state was standing right there on the beach next to the hangdog native, an idiot's grin plastered across his face as he handed over a giant check with "EIGHT BILLION SIMOLEONS" printed across it, and Uncle Sucker's John Hancock scribbled down the bottom.

"You want in on the deal, just call Shyster, Pilfer and Fraud. I got their 800 number on some promotional cocktail napkins their delivery boy just dropped off. Some creep in a towel with wings on his hat."

"I think, Ed, that I am just going to call it a day. There's just so much stupid one man can take, and I've suddenly bagged my limit."

I slugged down my one drink and took off for the door as Jaublowski resumed digging around behind the bar.

When I pulled open the door, a scrawny little guy in a disco-era outfit nearly knocked me down as he stumbled in from the daylight. He was only about five-five, and he looked up at me and blinked away the sun as he absorbed the gloom.

"Hey, you. Get outta here, ya bum!" Jaublowski bellowed out behind me. "Lousy deadbeat's been coming in here since last week. Ain't got a pot to piss in, and keeps ordering ambrosia. Like I got that fancy-ass pantheistic stuff in a joint like this."

The little disco bastard recoiled when he finally made out my smiling face. He was the kind who'd hit a guy when he was down, and he must have figured I was too.

I stepped back and magnanimously motioned for the shrimp to pass.

"Set my buddy up, Ed," I called. "Put it on my tab."

The little old bum didn't need to be given the green light twice. He hustled away from me on fleet feet and over to the bar. I heard him say one thing in a pipsqueaky voice as Jaublowski poured out a tumbler of something that was definitely not ambrosia.

"I was a god once. A *god,*" he insisted as he slobbered desperately around the rim of his glass.

"Ain't it the truth," I called over to the pair of them.

The little twerp was too busy slugging down the barkeep's newest watered-down paint thinner to even hear me. Only Jaublowski looked up. The miserable bastard bartender was wearing a quizzical expression at my non sequitur as he lazily wiped a grimy rag around the filthy bar.

"What're you talking about, Jinx?"

I shrugged in the doorway. "That we've all got our crosses to bear."

I strolled back out into the sunlight, leaving the two new pals to annoy the hell out of each other in the cheerful gloom of O'Hale's Bar.

A Note from Jim Mullaney

If you enjoyed this book, please take a moment to post a positive review at Amazon, and spread the news at your personal web site, Facebook page, etc. I don't know if these simple kindnesses will get you into Heaven, but they might help to keep the author out of the unemployment line.   — *Jim Mullaney*

Other books by Jim Mullaney

The Crag Banyon Mysteries series:

One Horse Open Slay
Devil May Care
Royal Flush
Sea No Evil
Bum Luck
Flying Blind
Shoot the Moon
The Butler Did I.T.
X is For Banyon
Sleep Tight, Wake Dead
Habeas a Nice Corpus
Banyon Investigations, Inc. (*Crag Banyon anthology*)

The Red Menace series:

Red and Buried
Drowning in Red Ink
Red the Riot Act
A Red Letter Day
Red on the Menu
Red Devil

About the author

James Mullaney is a Shamus Award-nominated author of over 40 books, as well as comics, short stories, novellas, and screenplays. His work has been published by New American Library, Gold Eagle/Harlequin, Marvel Comics, Tor, Moonstone Books, and Bold Venture Press. He was ghostwriter and later credited writer of 26 novels in *The Destroyer* series, and wrote the series companion guide *The Assassin's Handbook 2*. He is currently the author of *The Red Menace* action series as well as the comic-fantasy *Crag Banyon Mysteries* detective series.

He was born in Taxachusetts, and wishes he were an only child, save one.